John L

The Man — The Miracle

Merry Christmas
2020

Kent Weatherby

Disclaimer and Acknowledgments

Lazarus Alive: The Man —The Miracle is a work of fiction
prompted by names, descriptions, entities, and incidents
relating to the lives of real people as described in the Bible
first published as Rising from Bethany: the Story of Lazarus
(now out of print). The story is told from an Old Testament
point of view. Lazarus had only the Torah, the writing of the
prophets, the history and poetry to guide him. His quest to
find the Messiah was hampered by uncertainty and doubt.
Was John the Baptist the Messiah and if not he then who?
Lazarus is surrounded by doubters and scoffers, those
following false religion and a political-religious hierarchy
threatened by the appearance of the One the people had for
centuries longed to see. But when he finds a carpenter from
Nazareth who does the things prophesied for the Messiah he
is confused by talk of death and dying. By becoming the
miracle Lazarus at last finds the Savior he has been seeking.

Introduction

The story of Lazarus has fascinated generations of people. In that historical event Jesus built on his promise of eternal life. He had preached about the difference between our temporal existence with pain, suffering, and physical death, comparing it to the promise of eternity with Him. He had spoken of a spiritual life where those who had died lived real lives with real bodies in the presence of God. His listeners often misunderstood.

As He anticipated his final days on earth, both God and man, he took the lesson a giant step forward. He demonstrated his power over physical death. By restoring Lazarus to life He prepared His followers for the gospel message revealed on Resurrection Sunday. By that miracle He proved that he had not only power over physical death but through Him we have eternal life. But what kind of body did Lazarus have? Was it an earthly physical body or was it a resurrected body? The Bible does not tell us.

As Christians, we believe that the Bible is the true and inerrant word of God. Jesus said that Lazarus died, but what became of him after his resurrection? In both the Catholic and Orthodox tradition Lazarus lived on to become a bishop of the church in either France or Cyprus, where he died again. But did he really go to one of those distant places? If so, how do we reconcile his supposed later death with

Hebrews 9:27-28: "And just as it is destined that men die only once, and after that comes judgment, so also Christ died only once as an offering for the sins of many people; and he will come again, but not to deal again with our sins. This time he will come bringing salvation to all those who are eagerly and patiently waiting for him."

Jesus could not have made it any plainer than he did at John 11:14-15: "Lazarus is dead. And for your sake, I am glad I wasn't there, for this will give you another opportunity to believe in me. Come, let's go to him."

Chapter 1

"Lazarus, come forth!" The man hearing those words had died four days earlier at mid-morning during the month of Adar in the year 3788 following a short illness. The dead man recognized the voice. It was the same voice that spoke the words, "Let there be light." The words were spoken by his good friend, Jesus of Nazareth. That was why he had been born. That was his destiny, the reason Jesus had singled him out for a special miracle. This was why he had not been included in the Twelve or sent out with the Seventy.

His sisters Mary and Martha buried him before sundown in accordance with the Law of Moses and their custom. God's will! He had been in good health when he returned home four weeks earlier accompanied by his friend. But after that friend left people in his village noticed how rapidly his health deteriorated. Some in the small village wondered what caused the man to die. Most were certain. He died from apoplexy— the same condition that killed his father. If so, it had also killed Uzzah during the reign of King David as he steadied the Ark of the Covenant to keep it from falling.

The day he lapsed into a coma his sisters sent word to his friend to come quickly before he died, but the friend had failed to do so. The illness had been of short duration—not more than a few days—and the friend had not been far away. He could have come. Why had he not done so?

At the tomb carved into the rock of the Bethany hill they rolled the heavy stone across the entrance to the tomb and recited Kaddish the prayer for the dead. They prayed not so much for their departed brother as for the dead nation that had drifted so far away from the God of their fathers. Then they slowly, sorrowfully walked away with the sun slipping below the brow of the rocky hill. The dead man and his family had been part of the Hebrew sect that believed in more than the misty afterlife of contemporary Jewish culture. They believed in the resurrection of the body but in this hour of grief the family could not imagine what that meant.

For the dead man's sisters it was about the ritual. Returning to their home beyond the crest of the hill known as the Mount of Olives they prepared for Shivah the seven-day period of mourning in which they received visitors. The days passed slowly for them, often sitting with friends without talking for hours at a time. The women focused on their individual feelings, reconciling themselves to the death of their brother. They tried to imagine how they would ever resume a normal life without him. All the while they sat in silence the sisters pondered what they believed to be a senseless death.

On the fourth day following the entombment a family friend rushed into the house. Ignoring custom and the usual greeting made during the period of mourning—"May the Omnipresent comfort you among the other mourners of Zion and Jerusalem"—he shouted, "He's coming!" Nothing more was needed. Everyone in the house knew what he meant. They knew the man coming was Jesus of Nazareth, the friend who had tarried when called days earlier.

Now, also ignoring the custom of the Jews, Martha rushed out of the house and down the dusty path. She ran through the village in the direction of the Jericho road where she would confront the man who could have saved her brother's life. In the depth of her despair she rushed up to him as he approached at a furious pace. Breathless, the faith she had in the man spilled out. "Sir, if you had been here, my brother wouldn't have died. By now the smell will be terrible, for he has been dead four days." The words carried the raw emotions the middle-aged woman felt. Jesus saw her despair, and being deeply moved in spirit, felt compassion for her loss. Tears came to Jesus' eyes. She loved her brother. She loved him too yet her words carried a tone of accusation. Deep within the recess of her mind, she thought: Why did you not come when we sent word, and you were not far off. Those words were never spoken. Instead, she continued, removing the sting of her thoughts, "Even now I know that whatever You ask of God, God will give You."

The man looked at her with sorrow in his heart for the pain she felt. He had known this time would come when he stayed away. It grieved him to cause her pain, hearing the unspoken words as clearly as the audible ones, but he also knew that her faith would sustain her. "Your brother will rise again," he answered.

"I know he will rise again in the resurrection at the last day."

Martha knew the words but not the meaning. It was the lesson the man had come to teach. Only by waiting for his friend to die could he accomplish his purpose. And even then, the full import of the lesson would not be understood for another five weeks. The proximity of Bethany and Jerusalem assured that word of the miracle he came to perform could spread. For the man and his purpose that was important. In the presence of Martha and the twelve men accompanying him on the long walk over the mountainous terrain, he answered, "I am the resurrection and the life. He who believes in me will live, even though he dies; and whoever lives and believes in me will never die. Do you believe this?"

"Yes, Lord; I have believed that You are the Christ, the Son of God, even He who comes into the world." She spoke the words easily but her eyes betrayed the lack of comprehension.

Jesus smiled at her, his eyes filled with pity. He looked to his right and saw the cemetery "Where have you laid him?" he asked.

She answered, gesturing in the direction of the tomb, "Just here; come and see."

Jesus placed his hand on her shoulder to comfort her

and looked into the eyes that expressed hope and trust. He also saw confusion, but not doubt. "Martha, go and bring Mary here, and the truth of the resurrection will be revealed to you."

As she left Martha saw the men traveling with Jesus sitting in groups of two and three with one of the men sitting alone a short distance away from the others. Martha knew they were all strong men who had walked hundreds of miles following the man they called Master. But they were now tired from the furious pace set for them as they had approached Bethany.

Minutes later the two sisters returned hurrying along the road in the company of the people who came to grieve with them. No one spoke. They waited uncertain what would happen. Then Jesus stood before the tomb, prayed silently and spoke the words, "Lazarus, come out!" The sisters now standing near the entrance strained to see inside the dark tomb holding veils over their faces to mask the smell of decay. At first nothing, then a faint sound as if someone had moved from within. Martha took a hesitant step forward her heart pounding uncertain what would happen next. Something moved at the bottom of the stone steps leading to the inner chamber. She did not think, could not think. She moved back as the apparition slowly emerged constrained by its grave clothes. The apparition she had once known as her brother moved past her, sightless with the grave napkin still covering its eyes until it stopped directly in front of Jesus, not more that an arm length away.

Jesus said to those nearest him, "Unwrap him and let him go!"

The men, followers of Jesus standing nearby, held back. One was heard to comment, "But if we touch the man, we will be unclean."

"The man we know and love whose name is Lazarus is not dead, as you can plainly see. He is not unclean. Nor will you be if you do as I say," Jesus replied. "Nevertheless, here is water in a well just down the hill. After you have done as I asked, go and wash. Then, on the third day, wash again. On the seventh day, you will be clean. I tell you to do this so that you will fulfill the letter of the Law."

Thomas reluctantly stepped forward, followed by Bartholomew, a man Jesus sometimes playfully called Barley after the grain that grew in the fields of Israel. But now he was not called Barley. Bartholomew was called upon by his Master to do something that sent waves of revulsion through him. Repulsed by the smell of death coming from the tomb the two men reached out with trembling hands for the burial cloth. With their eyes cast away from the abomination, they began to slowly unwind the binding from the body standing before them. As they did so, the stench of death dissolved until the smooth, olive-skinned body of the middle-aged Jewish man was revealed, absent any sign of death or decay.

Their pace quickened as they realized that they had been asked to participate in a miracle—not just observe but actually be a physical part of it.

Lazarus blinked squinting as he faced the morning sun. The bright light of the sun shined in his eyes, though the light was not as brilliant as the light he had seen just before he heard the voice. He wondered. How did I get out here? I have been ill, too sick to get up from my bed and now I am standing outside in the midst of a crowd in the cemetery with hardly any clothes on. How can that be?

Jesus smiled as would a parent proud of a son's accomplishment and said, "Come. Let's return to your house so that Mary and Martha can prepare breakfast for us. My companions and I have been on the road since early this morning and have had nothing to eat. And you, my friend, must be hungry after your ordeal."

The two women now came rushing forward. They threw themselves at Jesus' feet and cried out in thanksgiving. Then rising they embraced their brother. Laughing, they set off for the house once more a home.

Jesus walking beside his friend, hand on his shoulder, whispered in his ear. All anyone heard was the phrase, "Very soon everyone will know the truth you have seen. Then we will once again be together living beyond the grasp of time in glory."

On a day three and a half years earlier a man squinted over the parchment on the high table. His eyes were tired and his back ached from the strain of bending over his work. Over twenty hours had passed since he had risen that day to copy the writings of Israel's greatest prophet, Isaiah. He had finished copying the thirty-eighth and thirty-ninth chapters of the ancient manuscript. But when he reached chapter forty, he had felt compelled to continue working far past quitting time. The sun had set hours earlier, but the man had been so occupied with the completion of his task that he lit a lamp and continued long after his brothers in the community had retired for the night. This was not the first time John son of the priest Zacharias had copied the sacred scroll. Each of the brothers had taken turns in copying the scrolls, and it had been more than two years since he had last had the opportunity to work with the writings of Israel's greatest prophet.

John had just passed his thirtieth birthday although the passing of the day had not been noted by the community of Essenes. Such celebrations were alien to the men who lived and worked in this remote place. Qumran, the home of the Essenes, lay in the desert Judean hills some five hundred feet above the Dead Sea. He had lived and worked with the Essenes for eighteen years arriving as a boy of twelve when his mother and father died.

In the beginning, he had been given work as a domestic

helper in the monastic order, dedicated to an ascetic way of life while he completed his education. He had shown great promise and soon had been given the task of joining the scholars who worked with the scrolls. Now he had a respected place in the community and was recognized as one of the promising young men who one day might rise to lead the entire community. But John wondered if the life of a monk and scholar was the life he was meant to follow. He had been happy as the years passed but as he moved from age twenty-nine to thirty, a restless spirit had settled over him.

He had been excited when the leader of the community assigned him the task of copying Isaiah's scroll bearing the words. The project had been routine though exhilarating as he worked his way through the first thirty-nine chapters. Every time he copied the words, they seemed to speak to him. But this time, when he reached the fortieth chapter of the prophecy something happened. It was not just words he copied. Now it seemed to him that a voice was speaking directly to him. He paused to read what he had just written. He heard a sound like rustling leaves. What leaves? Qumran stood on a desert plateau. There were no leaves. Then he thought he heard a voice speak:

Comfort my people. Speak tenderly to Jerusalem and tell her that her sad days are gone. Her sins are pardoned, and I have punished her in full for all her sins. Make a road for the Lord through the wilderness; make him a

straight, smooth road through the desert. Fill the valleys;
level the hills; straighten out the crooked paths, and
smooth off the rough spots in the road. The glory of the
Lord will be seen by all mankind together. Shout to
Jerusalem from the mountaintops! Shout louder—don't
be afraid—tell the cities of Judah, "Your God is coming!"
Had he read the words or had they been spoken to him?
Suddenly, he knew the answer. Just as the Holy Spirit had
been given to the prophets of old, the Spirit of God had now
been given to him. The words written by Isaiah were about
him. In that instant he knew that he must leave the comfort
and protection of the Essenes, but where he would go? Judah,
the voice said Judah. How would he accomplish this task? For
that, he would do just as those prophets of old had done. He
would trust his God.

He licked his fingers and pinched the wick floating in
the oil lamp. The room instantly plunged into darkness; but
in that darkness he could now see clearly for the first time in
his life. He walked from his stool to the door—a walk that
had not changed in fifteen years—and into the night, a starlit
night the likes of which he had never before witnessed. The
moon and stars were all he needed to find his way from the
library where the scrolls were copied to the dormitory where
all the brothers slept. He could hardly wait for morning when
he would meet with the leader of the community.

He slept little that night. His mind whirled with what he

now understood was his calling. He awoke at first light, rose and went to the communal room for prayer. Immediately following the morning prayers, he approached the man he had come to know almost as a father. "I am leaving," he said with an abruptness that startled the old man.

"Leaving? What are you talking about?"

"I am leaving the community."

The man stood still, shocked. "But why, where will you go? What will you do?"

John answered, "Why? I go because the Spirit of God has moved me to do so. Where? I will go where the Spirit leads me. What will I do? I will do whatever the Spirit tells me to do." He then related the revelation he had received the night before.

The older man stood listening, skeptical at first; but as John related the story, his visage softened. At last he said, "I knew there was something special about you from the time you first joined us. So this is it. Are you certain?"

"I have never been more certain of anything in my life. I will be leaving as soon as I can gather my belongings."

The men embraced as if they were father and son. A tear came into the old man's eye. "Go with God, and may he protect you. Something tells me you will need His protection."

While the others left the communal room to return to either the library where they worked or any one of a dozen other places of employment, John returned to the dormitory. He looked around at the sparse accommodations, the rough stone building partitioned into cubicles barely eight feet square, each containing only a cot for sleeping, some not even having an opening to let in fresh air. Only the density of the rock cooled the cubicle from the piercing desert heat. Never again will I enjoy such comfort as this, he thought. He left before noon and abandoned the monastic lifestyle for one of direct service to God and mankind. He walked down the twisting road that led to the valley floor. From there he struck out for the first of several towns located near the western shore of the salt lake. He went to the center of town and began preaching the words of Isaiah, now understanding what they meant in a new and more exciting way. He then went north along the Jordan River, baptizing those who came to hear his message, calling on them to repent of their sin and be cleansed. At first, there were no crowds following him so he watched and waited for groups of men and women to come to the river, the women to wash clothes, the men to water their animals. He engaged them in conversation explaining to them that the kingdom of God and the long awaited Messiah was in the world. He stayed near the towns so word of his presence could spread. When those in one town had heard him preach he moved on to the next village along the river until a group of people began traveling along with him drawing ever larger crowds to hear the message of hope and to be baptized in the River Jordan. His life was difficult and he was often hungry, living on whatever food others brought him or he found in the fertile land along the western bank of the river. As time passed, his appearance changed and his demeanor matched the zeal of his message. He no longer had to look for individuals. Great multitudes came looking for him and he moved to more remote locations.

Within six months his fame had spread across Judah and into Galilee and Perea. Everyone was talking about the man they now called the Baptist. Who was John the Baptist? Where was he? Was he the long-awaited Messiah? Everyone, the Temple leaders included, wanted to know.

In the village of Bethany outside of Jerusalem, a man and his sisters had not just asked these questions, they intended to find out for themselves. They had discussed the possibility of the brother making a trip to find John and hear firsthand the message he preached.

Chapter 2

The light of early dawn crept through the open doorway illuminating the hard-baked clay-tile floor and the relative luxury the family possessed. Befitting his station in life he had furnished the house with tables and benches, ornate pottery, clay vessels for storing food, woven baskets on the ground floor. Rugs covered the floor of two rooms. Upstairs in the sleeping-quarters wooded cots for sleeping, woolen blankets, a table that served double duty as a desk for doing his accounts, an oil lamp and shutters opened at the window completed the furnishings. The larger room on the ground floor was used only for their daily meals, special occasions, feasts, and entertaining on those rare occasions when the siblings were in a festive mood.

The evening before had been unusually warm for the time of year and Lazarus had left the wooden door ajar so that air could circulate in the two-story four-room house. Now the room felt cold. The house surrounded by a low-walled courtyard with the back of the house located against the rear wall faced east allowing the pink glow to spread across the floor and on to the cot where the man slept. His two sisters occupied the other top-floor room where they remained asleep. Blinking, he rubbed his eyes to remove the last matted barrier separating sleep and consciousness. He rose from where he lay and rolled up the soft lightweight wool blanket placing it at the head of his narrow bed, making the platform into a seat for the rest of the day. This was a big day for Lazarus and he moved quietly not wishing to awaken his sisters. He reflected how good it was to have them live with him especially after what the three of them had experienced in the past two years. He hurried down the outside stone stairway and entered the large room on the ground floor. He picked up the heavy clay water jug and carried it outside. He placed it on a wooden bench after first filling the shallow bowl used for washing. He splashed the cool water on his face and then dried his skin and beard using his outer garment as a towel. Hardworking, contemplative and devout by nature, Lazarus took life seriously. Mary and Martha were comfortable here, and it gave him pleasure to think that he had been able to provide for them. No longer a young man, though no one thought of him yet as old, Lazarus had celebrated his thirty-second birthday just weeks before. Friends and neighbors had noted his good fortune in assuming responsibility for the olive grove just over the top of the hill. The grove that had belonged to his father passed to him when the older man died suddenly of the illness known as apoplexy four years earlier. It had been the same illness that struck down his grandfather before Lazarus reached age six. His mother too was dead.

He reflected on the fact that God had blessed him but life had its sadness. His wife had died in childbirth leaving him without an heir. Then his two sisters had come to live with him. The comfortable life he led would have been empty without them. Both women had married early in life but they too had lost their spouses to illness. No kinsman existed to fulfill the responsibility of leaving an heir for the childless widows so it had fallen to Lazarus to take them into his own home. He took his responsibility seriously. Blessed, yes, but still he suffered. He wondered if these trials were punishment for the sin he knew to be part of his life. Lazarus longed for something, someone. He yearned for the day when he and the people of Israel would be complete, when they would know the full blessing of their God. He turned toward the west, toward Jerusalem and Mount Moriah where the Temple, the dwelling place of God where Abraham had been willing to sacrifice his son Isaac.

The people in Jerusalem referred to the high ground where his grove lay as a mountain, the Mount of Olives; but from his point of reference, it was nothing more than a small hill separating Bethany from the larger olive grove that lay four hundred feet above the Kidron Valley. The distance from his home located on the hill to the Eastern Gate of the walled city was just over a mile.

He stooped to tie the leather thong of his sandal. The rising sun warmed the crisp air as he thought to himself how spring would soon be upon them. He picked up the heavy water jug and walked down the hill toward the town a quarter of a mile distant. He knew that his sisters would appreciate this small gesture. The few servants he employed never seemed to arrive in time to perform this difficult task leaving it to the two women. The small women would be relieved to know the job of carrying the six-gallon jug back up the hill had been done. The jug itself weighed nearly ten pounds when empty. Filled, it meant that either Mary or Martha had to carry the sixty-pound load, three-fourths their body weight, back up the hill from the well to the house. He hurried as he walked up the hill, hardly aware of the heavy burden. Lazarus was, after all, a strong man accustomed to work.

He had a long way to travel. He had heard about a man preaching in the wilderness and wanted to see for himself. That meant that he would have to walk down the Jericho Road from Bethany into the Jordan rift, a risky journey when traveling alone. He had asked but there was no one else he knew interested in making the trip. Lazarus gave thanks that he did not have the appearance of a man possessing great wealth. He took comfort in knowing that, although he did live comfortably, he had the good judgment to never flaunt the fact by his mode of dress or action. The Jericho Road had a reputation of being fertile ground for thieves and murderers. Lazarus could only recall a handful of times when he had made the trip. On those occasions he had been accompanied by others and he had always offered a prayer of thanksgiving when he arrived safely at the end.

Mary and Martha were outside waiting for him when he arrived back at the house. They smiled as they watched him stride up the steep path. They loved him for all the good things he did for them. "When will you be leaving?" Mary asked.

"Where will you go?" Martha joined in.

The two sisters knew that their brother intended to look for the man John in the country bordering the Jordan River.

"I don't know," he responded, answering only Martha's question. "It is said that he is somewhere north of the Dead Sea." He reflected on the desolation of the place the Greeks had named Asphaltites, a place so devoid of life that the salty water supported no living thing. It was a dead sea a place so low that it remained warm even in the depth of winter. "I will go to Jericho and ask if anyone knows where John is preaching. I will then go wherever they tell me."

Lazarus paused to consider the arrangements he had made concerning the olive grove during his absence. Most of the seasonal work had been completed. The time was right for him to be away for several days. The young men he employed could easily handle the limited work that remained unfinished. Seeing the look of concern on his sisters' faces, he continued. "I should leave now. The road to Jericho is over twenty miles long and it is dangerous. Remember, we heard about the man attacked by robbers. He lay by the side of the road for a day before anyone would help him. I want to be at the bottom before night." He said this not to worry them but to reassure them that he would not take any chances. "Once I get to the Jordan River valley, I will be safe. Besides, at this time of day I should be able to catch up to some merchant and travel with his caravan. It is unlikely a group of men would be set upon by thieves."

The sisters nodded in agreement relieved that their brother had a plan. The reckless streak he had shown as a boy worried them. As a man he had matured, and they knew he had good judgment. Only the headaches he experienced from time to time caused them any worry. And those, when they did come, led him to his bed where he suffered in silence. They knew that he could be relied upon to do nothing to place himself in jeopardy.

Martha hurried to gather some of yesterday's bread and figs from the pottery jar. These she placed in the leather pouch Lazarus would carry over his shoulder and across his body to make it more difficult for someone to wrench it from him—just in case.

They watched him retie the thong of his sandal and gird his coarse wool outer garment using a broad leather belt. As a final act of preparation he braided his long brown hair into a single knot. It would be cooler that way once he reached the searing heat of the Jordan rift. Minutes later with the sun still low in the early morning light, he picked up the wooden staff that would serve as both an aid in walking and a weapon then departed. The two women stood beyond the courtyard outside the low wall watching as he walked with strong even steps down the hill toward Bethany. They had no way to know that the place where it intersected the path to Jericho was a metaphor for their life.

Lazarus walked with the steady gait of a man accustomed to traveling by foot. The staff in his right hand pumped in rhythm each time his left leg strode forward. The power it gave his pace moved him along well beyond what he could have done without the aid. Average in height, his five-and-a-half-foot frame would take many steps on the twenty-mile journey. He was thankful that the trip would be downhill, three quarters of a mile to an elevation below sea level at Jericho.

The road leading from Jerusalem through Bethany and on to Jericho began as a broad highway at the royal city of David, the seat of temporal and spiritual power of all Judea and Palestine for the Jews. It narrowed as it proceeded toward the east. By the time Lazarus had walked just over a mile beyond Bethany it ceased being a road at all. It narrowed even more a mile later when it became a ten-foot-wide dirt trail packed by the feet of a thousand camels, donkeys, horses, and humans. Slowly, that too disintegrated until it was nothing more than a desert mountain path twisting and turning first down and then up but inexorably leading lower toward the Jordan rift.

He walked alone confident that he could fight off one or two bandits with his staff. If there were more than that he would rely on speed to escape. He had always been fleet of foot and could outrun any who might lie in wait. He walked these first two miles without worry. He was still too close to the town for thieves to be lurking in the rocks around a bend in the road. Still, it would be comforting to have the company of an early caravan which may have passed through Bethany unnoticed as he made his final preparation for the journey. He had walked less than an hour when he saw them ahead, a merchant with five heavily laden donkeys and three men, traveling slowly winding down the path a quarter of a mile ahead. They had reached the first steep place on the descent, a place where the path switched back on itself as it made its way down the exposed rock cliff. Lazarus quickened his pace.

As he hurried to catch up to them he saw the man at the end of the procession look over his shoulder, watching. When Lazarus approached within shouting distance, he called out, "Shalom." He meant them no harm and wanted them to understand. They slowed slightly but remained wary of a trap. The call had come just as the caravan reached a bend in the path a perfect place for an ambush. Lazarus stopped fifty yards short of the merchant who had now lagged behind his companions. Lazarus held up his right hand, palm open, as a greeting and to show he did not pose any danger. The man responded in like manner. Lazarus moved forward, slowly now, so the man would have no cause for alarm and call his servants to come to his aid.

"Shalom," Lazarus repeated as he reached the merchant. "May I join your caravan? I am alone and have heard stories of travelers being attacked, robbed, and left for dead. My name is Lazarus. I live on the hill outside Bethany."

"Welcome, friend." The merchant relaxed. "I am Nathan, a rug merchant. We will be happy for your company."

For the first time, Lazarus noticed the rugs. They appeared to be similar to one that covered the floor of his second-story room. He said nothing, not wanting to draw attention to even that small fact evidencing wealth.

The two men turned and walked toward the caravan of donkeys and young men, little more than boys, who waited just a few feet ahead. When they reached the others they all resumed their trek, each leading an animal and marking their steps on the uneven ground. Large, sharp rocks protruded up through the sparse soil. Soon, even the thin layer of soil disappeared and the road became nothing more than a rock-strewn path with steep cliffs where both man and beast could easily fall to their death.

An hour later they reached the bottom of this first obstacle. The sun stood midway between dawn and its zenith. With its ascendance and their descent the heat had risen. Dust rose from the feet of the men and beasts. They were soon all covered from their feet to above their knees with the gray-brown particles. The men sweating profusely were thankful for the lack of strong wind, knowing that otherwise their faces and nostrils would also be clogged with the fine grit. Their breathing would then have been turned into a labored gasp through a mask of mud.

From time to time a slow-moving caravan passed them going up the mountainous road in the direction they had come. Wary greetings were exchanged with those who were Jewish. For the others only fearful recognition marked the passage. Those who did not share in their faith were viewed with suspicion. Lazarus knew that he had been fortunate to join with the merchant. Alone, he would have been easy prey for these people as well as for the more traditional bandit.

Two hours after the sun had been directly overhead, the caravan stood at the top of a second high cliff, steeper and more treacherous than the first. Here, there was not so much a threat of bandits but of falling. The cliff rose over a thousand feet above a fertile valley where citrus fruit, oranges, lemons, beans, lentil, tomatoes, and other produce grew in abundance. The town that prospered on the high ground beside the river above flood level was their destination: Jericho.

The small caravan began its descent from the precipice. The men could not help but see the beauty of the valley below. Green and lush, with fruit trees and palms, green grass, and colorful fabric floating with the breeze from balconies, Jericho could be seen in the distance still hundreds of feet below. It filled Lazarus with awe but frightened him at the same time. He saw groups of men, sometimes with animals, carefully picking their way up the narrow path. He wondered how they could pass a large caravan of animals on the way up. Where would they find a safe place to pass without someone being forced off the path and over the steep cliff? He thought. If we must pass someone on the way up let us cling to the cliff wall.

"We must be very careful here," the merchant remarked to Lazarus. "The animals are tired, and so are we. A false step here will result in our death and the shadowy grave."

Lazarus acknowledged the danger but marveled at the man's lack of understanding and faith. "I would not want to fall from this height, but the grave holds little terror for me. I believe God will provide and the grave is only temporary."

The man looked at Lazarus but held his tongue.

Chapter 3

Where Bethany was a village, Jericho was a city. A great walled city, the oldest city ever built by the hand of man had once stood at the location. It was here that the Hebrew people after forty years of wandering in the wilderness as punishment for disobedience finally crossed the Jordan River to occupy the land promised to their father Abraham two thousand years earlier. Lazarus knew the story of how God had performed a miracle for his people by using Joshua and the Hebrew army to defeat the defenders in the walled city of Jericho. Like all the Jews he thrilled at the telling of the story, how the people had marched around the city seven times before the sound of a ram's horn brought down the walls. Over the centuries, the city had been rebuilt and destroyed countless times. Nothing remained visible above ground to testify to existence of the early city. Its glory was gone. The new city's inhabitants, as were those in Bethany, subject to the nominal protection and humiliation of the Roman legions garrisoned east of the Jordan River.

The merchant called to his servants, boys really, telling them to take a tight grip on their donkey's rope harness. Then, exchanging control of beasts with Lazarus, he explained, "The other animals have made this trip before. The one you have been leading is only a yearling. This is her first trip. The feeling of air below may cause her to be skittish. It is best that I lead her. You follow the boys and I will follow you. That way the poor animal may be comforted by walking in the tracks of others."

Lazarus cast a nervous glance down as took his turn on the narrow path. The great distance and the feeling of air beneath him upset his equilibrium. After that he followed the merchant's advice and looked only at the rear of the animal in front and the rocky path beneath his feet. The men hugged the cliff wall fearing an animal would become frightened knocking them over the edge. The steep path reeked from the excrement and urine of the thousand beasts that had trod the way before them. Not even a breeze on this still day could dissipate the awful stench.

Near the bottom the second boy in line wandered outside his donkey while reversing direction at a switchback. He stumbled and fell dragging his beast with him over the edge. After tumbling a short distance the donkey came to rest on top of the boy. A moment later he called out. "I am not hurt." Embarrassed by the fall and his failure to heed his master's warning the boy rejoined the caravan where a new boy took charge of his donkey and the caravan continued on its journey to the valley floor six hundred feet below sea level.

Only when they reached the valley an hour later did the men relax their muscles, releasing the tension in their necks and backs. For Lazarus, the tension threatened the onset of one of his headaches.

He now became aware of the oppressive heat. Up until then the fear of falling had suppressed all other senses. He saw the ripples heat created in the air. It had been hot since midday when the sun beat down on them as they descended the heights, but now a new kind of heat punished them. Water from the river Jordan mixed with the super-heated air made breathing difficult. He was relieved to be safely at the bottom of the Jordan rift. Ready to begin his quest to find the man they called the Baptist he walked to the center of town just as the shadow from the high cliff crept across the ground. He saw merchants in the market emerging from their afternoon respite opening their stalls. He found a greater variety of food than he had ever seen at home. Most spectacular were the oranges, so large he could barely hold one in the palm of his hand. He reached into a pouch hanging from his belt and extracted his money, five shekels broken into agora coins of various denominations.

He stopped before making a purchase, considering the needs of his body, then purchased a small piece of roasted goat meat from a vendor. He smiled inwardly, knowing he had chosen wisely. Earlier in the day, the man would not have bargained so easily for the meat. From another, he bought a small quantity of hummus. Last of all, he bought one of the large citrus fruits. He then found a location near the market well where he could sit on the ground and eat. He drew fresh,

cool water from the well and dropped in the shade beside the
rock wall. He felt the evaporating sweat cool his body. He
bowed his head and gave thanks to the giver of all things, first
for a safe journey and then for the provision of nourishment.
Only then did his hunger overwhelm him. He eagerly
devoured the meat, eating it with some of the flat bread
packed by his sisters, dipping it in the hummus flavored by a
hot, red spice made from chilies. He followed that with a few
of the dried figs. Finally, as a treat, he peeled the orange and
reveled in the taste. The entire meal had cost him three agora.
Now knowing that food could be obtained for a reasonable
price, Lazarus realized he would have no trouble in sustaining
himself in the river valley until he found the man he sought.

Returning to the stalls, he asked the merchants where he
might find the man called John. Everyone answered with
certainty. They all gave directions, but each a different one.
One said to go here, another there. When he pressed them,
they each admitted they had never actually seen him; nor did
they know anyone who had. After wandering the market area
for an hour, Lazarus gave up, realizing that the people he
questioned were too busy with the demands of daily life to
have any interest in the promises of an itinerant preacher. He
left the market and struck out once more. This time, he
walked south, away from the paradise that Jericho represented
toward the desolation of the Dead Sea. He would go to the
colony of Essene at Qumran on the western bank of the river

another ten miles distant.

Harsh as the landscape had been on the way from Bethany to Jericho, it hardly prepared the pilgrim for what he found. He had heard stories about the wilderness below the ford that crossed the Jordan River but he was not prepared for the reality. The starkness of the country caused him to marvel that any group of people would choose to live in such a desolate wilderness. The road, a hard-packed surface free of stones, followed the river now over a hundred feet wide. The river, once clear and swift, now flowed sluggishly toward a place where the oppressive heat bore down on him like a wet cloth pressed over his face, making it nearly impossible to breathe. That place Lazarus knew was the Dead Sea. He walked steadily now and with purpose. He carried a full water skin, and he had sufficient food to last several days if he was careful. The question remained would one of the brothers at the Qumran community know where he could find him? He felt certain that they would tell him where, if they knew, even though John had abandoned his studies and work there.

Dust coated his feet and lower legs. He longed for a cool breeze but none came. He looked forward to night when his thirst would slake and he could conserve his water. After all, once he reached the saline sea, there were few places where he could get more in this land of dark ground encrusted with the white salts from the water below. Lazarus marveled at the location of a lake so remote that all the water flowing into it from the great Jordan River lay stagnant to evaporate leaving a surreal landscape.

He stopped for a minute on high ground with the saltwater sea visible now, sterile and dead. The sheltering cliffs above Jericho had curved far to the west, leaving him exposed to the heat of the sun. He wondered if a curse from God had formed the place. It was here that Moses wrote the cities of Sodom and Gomorrah had been destroyed in a terrible explosion? Now, out of this forsaken country seemingly accursed, John came preaching a message of repentance before God judged mankind. Even more importantly, John foresaw the fulfillment of God's promised Messiah who would deliver Israel from her suffering.

He walked for an hour with thoughts of great men's deeds racing though his head. In the distance, he saw a cleft in the cliff, less high than at Jericho leading to a waterfall, one of the few places he could get fresh water. It was the place where David, in the days before he became king, had spared the life of Saul, Israel's first king. King David. Yes, it was David whose house would produce the Messiah. Did John say anything about that? Lazarus had to know for certain. The place he saw was called En Geddi. Near that he would find the Essenes, but he still had many miles to travel. His pace slowed. The loneliness of the place sapped his energy. Then, in the distance, he saw a solitary man walking up the gently inclining road in his direction. He sat and waited. A half hour later, the man approached. While still some distance away, Lazarus saw by the man's dress that he was Jewish, not Bedouin. The closer he came Lazarus could see his manner of dress was not only Jewish but also expensive. A man of some wealth approached but he was alone, unusual in this wild country. He observed the man's beard, styled not merely cut, his hair worn in a mix of Jewish and Roman culture. Both the clothes and hair bespoke a man who had been traveling for some time and had not been able to attend properly to his appearance. He carried a shoulder bag larger than the one Lazarus had, evidence he had been away from his home for a considerable time.

"Shalom, brother," Lazarus greeted the man.

"And to you, brother," the man replied.

Lazarus extended the welcome customary to his people. "I have water if you thirst."

"You are kind." The man took the skin and drank, but only a drop. "Are you hungry?" he asked.

"I have eaten in Jericho only a few hours ago. It is not far. My name is Lazarus, from Bethany, near the Holy City. What is your destination?"

"I am Judas a pilgrim from Gamala, east of the Jordan River and south of Damascus. I am traveling from Qumran. My father sent me in search of the man John called the Baptist. Have your heard of him?"

"I have," Lazarus answered. "I too am traveling to see

the same man but do not know where he is. It is said he is somewhere near the Jordan River, but it is a great river coming from Mt. Hermon all the way to the Dead Sea. What have you heard?" He continued to eye the man before him, the same height but thinner. He has the soft hands of a man who does not do hard work, Lazarus observed. He had just been thinking about Qumran, En Geddi, and David. Could this man's sudden appearance be a sign from God that his quest was ordained?

The pilgrim shrugged. "Not much. It is said he may be found in the wilderness north of Jericho, along the bank of the river. Had I known that, I would not have traveled down to this place, a place without beauty. It is said he has been going up and down the river, preaching. If we go in that direction, we will surely encounter the crowds."

"It is settled then. I will go north, and if it is God's will, we can travel together." At last, Lazarus knew where to go.

Judas answered, "Ah, yes. It is certainly agreeable to me."

That settled, they turned north toward Jericho and walked back up the barren road. Not even a common serpent ventured out in the heat of the day. Only an occasional scorpion could be seen scurrying for shelter under a stone, where refuge or a meal might be found. Evening found them in the town where they located an inn. Before settling down for the night, they agreed to leave at first light. Providence works in strange ways, Lazarus thought. Just when he decided to go in the wrong direction, God had placed a man in his path, a man who spoke with authority, knowing the way to find John.

An hour before the dawn, Lazarus' traveling companion called out, "Wake up, my friend."

Lazarus awakened with a snort. "Huh? What is it?"

"You have slept soundly," Judas replied, only half joking. "No one could ever mistake your sleep for death. You snore too loudly."

Lazarus smiled but did not respond, thinking: Possibly I snored late in the night because you kept me awake with your infernal snoring earlier. Instead, he answered, "Perhaps it was because I was dreaming. Let me tell you about it." With that, he related the dream.

"It began when I was torn between two locations. Someone called to me from a long way off. After a short but difficult journey, I arrived at a destination I did not recognize but where I felt strangely at home. After a short while, a second voice commanded me to rise from my rest in my new home and return to my former home. I had found peace there and did not want to rise. The second voice was so compelling that I did. When I did, I discovered that the trip back where I had originated was not a difficult one at all. I wondered at how a journey could be so hard in one direction yet so easy in the other. Then I recalled how the trip down from Jericho had been relatively easy although harrowing because of the height. I knew that the trip back up would be hard. I wondered if my dream was confused by the reality of the climb ahead. Then, falling once more into a deep slumber, I heard the voice of the second person talking to me as a friend, but it was the voice of someone I don't know. Then I was awakened by you calling me just now. What can such a dream mean? Who were these people who called to me, pulling me this way and that, back and forth, and why? What do you make of it? It is troubling, but I cannot make any sense of why it should be."

"I don't know. Perhaps it has something to do with John. Some dreams have significance if they come from God. Others are nothing more than the result of a troubled mind that often leads us astray."

"I agree," Lazarus responded, "but I have nothing to trouble my mind other than the uncertainty of where we will find John. As for God he has never spoken to me and if he did I fear I would die on the spot."

His companion laughed. "I think I might do the same. Why should God talk to either one of us? Who are we to merit His concern? Doesn't He have enough to do just taking care of all His people? He talks through the prophets and priests. Surely Israel is far too important for Him to be concerned about two travelers, even though they may be far from home."

"Still, I would like to understand the dream. Maybe in time it will make sense. I have never had such a dream as this. It must have meaning."

They gathered their possessions and entered the large common room of the inn where the inn keeper had laid out fruit and bread for those departing early. Both men ate sparingly. The journey on foot once the sun rose high in the sky would be uncomfortable especially if they ate too much. Before setting out they made a last stop at the well. There they filled their goat water skins and washed their hair and beards. Less than a half hour after rising they were prepared to be on their way. Looking toward the east across the river they saw the first pink and yellow glow of light that promised the approach of a new day. The men walked south out of Jericho. Lazarus questioned his companion concerning what the Essenes had said.

He answered, "His brothers at Qumran told me that when he left them he intended to go into the wilderness along the east side of the Jordan River. They believe he may have intended to make the area around Bethabara his home. That is the place where I planned to begin my search."

Lazarus replied, "I do not know Bethabara. Do you know the way?"

"I do. It is not far."

The two men walked south retracing their steps until the road turned east. They crossed the river at the ford once used by Joshua and followed a road along the eastern bank of the river. When they reached their destination they learned John had gone north.

They then turned north retracing their steps and walked along the valley road just above the broken ravines forged by the rampaging river during the spring floods. The road they followed had been laid out in ancient times. Now it was used by the Jews in order to avoid traveling through Samaria. The men walked through the villages of Gilead, villages whose names meant nothing to either man. Night found them at a place just south of the place where the Jabbok River joined the Jordan River.

As they prepared their camp, Lazarus spoke. "You have an illustrious name."

Judas answered, his voice carried a tone of resignation. "I cannot see Israel ever being blessed by my poor family. We resided for many generations in Judah in the town of Kerioth, but now we live at Gamala on the Yarmuk River under the Tetrarchy of Philip. Because we came from Kerioth, we have adopted the family name of Iscariot. My father and his father before him were all men of business. Who ever heard of such a man having any part in God's plan for humanity? That is reserved for the prophets and kings, the rich and powerful and the occasional soldier of course."

Lazarus could not help himself. He laughed. "So then you are telling me you are not the Lion of Judah that the

Scriptures tell us to watch for. Nevertheless your name signifies greatness. How did you come to leave Judah for Syria?"

"It is a difficult story for me to relate. My older brother made friends with men who were Zealots. When a Roman citizen was stabbed the Zealots were blamed and everyone known to be friendly to them was arrested. After that, we did not believe we could stay in Kerioth so we went to Gamala."

The fire at their campsite began to flicker as the spent fuel burned low. It had been Lazarus who gathered the material piled near the fire so they could stay warm during the night. He wondered if it would be enough. Judas stared at it as Lazarus rose from where they sat to gather more of the sparse vegetation that grew along the riverbank. He noticed his companion did not appear to think about such things. He has lived a privileged life no doubt, he thought. He returned to the rock when he finished and sat staring into the growing flame. Both men felt the warmth it provided. Lazarus commented. "You know, we are at a famous spot. It was very near this place where Jacob wrestled with the angel of God. The ford in the river just there," he said, pointing to a place, "must be the spot."

The night grew colder as time passed since the sun had set. The men lay down on the grass mats they made from foliage Lazarus had gathered along the river. Loosening their robes they curled up on their soft beds and were soon fast asleep.

The information the two pilgrims were following proved to be true. Near the end of the second day walking the men reached a ford in the river not far from Pella on the east and Beit She'an on the west where there was a slight peninsula created by a bend in the stream. Here the flow of the water slowed creating a still shallow pool suitable for baptism. The cliffs to the east dropped in height, no longer precipitous but still rocky. A natural amphitheater provided a perfect place for John to preach.

A large crowd had assembled at the location to hear John preach. Lazarus and Judas hurried down the hill but arrived too late. John had finished for the day. The movement of the crowd converged and expanded like a beating heart revealing the path taken by John as he walked toward the hills. Judas wearied by the days' walk stopped while Lazarus ran ahead hoping to get a look at the man they had walked so far to see. The brief glimpse he did catch of the man startled him. He knew the man would not have the appearance of the priests at the Temple but he struggled to understand what he saw. He considered his own modest clothing. John did not look like either he or Judas. From a distance he could only see the man's back, an outer garment made of some coarse material with a thick belt at least a full hand in width around his waist and his long black hair tied at the back. His stride was powerful and even showing his sunbaked legs as he walked toward the cliffs and caves, a place of solitude. Moments later, a handful of his closest disciples followed.

Lazarus hurried back and told his friend what he had seen. "He did not look like the Messiah. He would never be mistaken for a king."

Judas answered with disdain. "I've walked all the way from Gamala to En Geddi and halfway back for what; for this? My father did not send me for this. But since we are here, I suppose there is nothing else to do but wait until morning. If he returns we shall see what he has to say. If not, then I will take leave of you and cross back over the river and return home."

Once more, the two men prepared to spend a night in the open. This time they camped in the company of a large crowd, most from the region of Galilee. Most seemed amazed at the appearance of John. Others commented that he looked exactly as they had been told. Another man grumbled that John was a fraud. Lazarus found a group who were talking in excited voices about what they had heard. Not a word about his appearance passed their lips. John was a prophet in the nature of the great prophets Isaiah and Elijah, they asserted. The two groups, so united before they saw John, now had little in common. The groups physically separated as the division between their perspectives grew. The larger group looked forward to John returning the next day and hearing him explain scripture to them.

Lazarus wanted to hear what they all had to say. When at last he returned to his travel companion after listening to the smaller group, he commented. "They believe the messiah will be a man who will lead the people in a war against the Romans. I don't know. I can't see that man leading anyone into battle. But what if they are wrong about the messiah? "

The camp mood that night fell into despair. There was no shelter, little food, and no fuel for fires to warm those who had gathered. It promised to be a difficult night, but not for everyone.

A number of religious leaders who stood apart from the rest of the crowd departed as those who remained prepared to spend the night. A few of the leaders had come from as far away as Jerusalem to hear what they chose to believe was heresy preached by John. There would be no sleeping under the stars for these men of privilege. They now hurried off to the accommodations secured for them by their servants in Pella a half mile distant over the crest of a nearby hill. Lazarus and Judas watched as they rode away. Neither man spoke. They did not need to speak. Their faces spoke for them. A vast chasm separated these organizers of religion from the faith of the patriarchs. Listening as they trotted past, Lazarus heard them discuss among themselves what they had heard the crowd say: "Some people said he was the reincarnate Elijah. Others say he is another of the ancient prophets."

Lazarus overheard enough of these men's conversation to know that the men had not believed anything they heard from the mouth of John or these witnesses. The religious leaders had only come to this remote location to prove that their belief was correct—John was a lunatic and nothing more. He had quoted Scripture to them but they had not believed, choosing their traditions and their writings and interpretation over the wisdom of the prophets.

Lazarus looked at Judas to see if he had the same reaction to the attitude displayed by these so-called moral guides of Israel. He could not tell.

Chapter 4

Dawn broke early in the late spring morning. The sun cast its light on the flood-ravaged desolation along the eastern bank of the Jordan River before spreading rapidly across the face of Roman-occupied Palestine. Lazarus awoke with the light falling on his face as he lay on the ground facing toward the east, the direction of hope. A moment later his companions close to the river also stirred. Looking north, they saw the snowy peak of Mount Hermon over nine thousand feet high in the distance. The air held the chill of the night brought by the rushing water as it cascaded from the mountain on its journey to a stagnant death in the Dead Sea. Each small group organized itself for the purpose of washing in water that only days earlier had been snow on the peak.

"Do you think he will return?" It was Lazarus who spoke.

"I don't know. He left so suddenly after we arrived and walked away with such determination."

They looked around and saw a great multitude that grew by the minute as new arrivals settled in to wait. All had temporarily abandoned their obligations to wives and children, to family at large, and their villages just as they had. So compelling was their desire to see and hear John that many had thought little of what they were really doing. Knowing that he preached forgiveness of their sin through baptism, ritual washing in the river, they were willing to risk the commission of one more sin for which they would have to ask forgiveness. It was a price they were prepared to pay to hear the man preach.

For Lazarus and his friend this promised to be a day of fasting. They had eaten the last of their food the night before. After completing their morning wash they sat on the ground to wait while Lazarus tried not to be conspicuous. It did not work. Within minutes Judas had attracted a nearby group of men that offered to share what they had. Accepting the smallest portions the men ate, grateful for what they had received. As they did so, fast-trotting donkeys came into view carrying the black and white-robed Pharisees and Sadducees. In sharp contrast to the common folk at the river these men had carefully combed beards. Ringlets of hair hung before their ears that they twirled muttering to themselves in a manner designed to draw attention to their coming more than testify to any piety.

Suddenly a voice called out, "He is coming back from the wilderness."

The massive crowd turned to see who had called out recognizing that the voice had come from the area farthest removed from the river. It had been in the opposite direction of the approaching religious leaders. In the distance Lazarus could make him out, a solitary figure striding with purpose over the rough terrain coming toward the river. The crowd alive to the prospect of seeing and hearing John also turned to see for themselves. The act of turning away from the men riding the donkeys to face the approaching Baptist carried with it a symbolism that struck Lazarus. The crowd seemed to be turning their back on the old religion. Seeing the crowd's reaction the men spurred on their animals. They had all heard about John, how he dressed and looked. Still, not one of those who had arrived during the night was prepared for the apparition that approached. He could not possibly have looked more different than the men on donkeys. It was not just his outward physical appearance. He had nothing on his head and his long free hair, uncut since birth in the style of a Nazirite like the ancient judge Samson, flowed down his neck. He wore a reddish brown robe made of coarse camel hair that hid the outward signs of dust from the wilderness. In contrast, the soft wool black robes of the religious leaders were covered in dust as they bounced on the backs of their donkeys. The contrast to the others was striking. The ornate headdresses they wore bespoke an additional mark of distinction that John obviously felt unnecessary. Where he was lean and hardened by a sparse diet, eating only what the wilderness provided, they were soft and fat by comparison. Where his skin was dried and darkened by the desert wind and sun theirs was olive-colored, smooth, and oiled. Where he would surely smell clean from the frequent washing in the river, they would be perfumed against the odor of their indulgent lifestyle.

John quickened his pace as he neared the crowd. Lazarus looked back at the approaching religious leaders. Another contrast became apparent. The men on donkeys were followed by a large retinue of servants, both male and female, little more than slaves who doted on their every desire. John on the other hand came accompanied by a small group of his followers, disciples, some who had camped by the river with the multitude. These men did not so much serve John as work with him. They now walked beside though just slightly behind John. They were helpers not servants, deferring to their leader. John walked through the crowd toward a large rock at the edge of the water. He paused, turned, and faced the religious leaders. In a firm voice, he said, 'You sons of snakes! Who said that you could escape the coming wrath of God? Before being baptized, prove that you have turned from sin by doing worthy deeds. Don't try to get by as you are, thinking: We are safe for we are Jews—descendants of Abraham. That proves nothing. God can change these stones here into Jews! And even now the ax of God's judgment is poised to chop down every unproductive tree. They will be chopped and burned. With water I baptize those who repent of their sins; but someone else is coming, far greater than I am, so great that I am not worthy to carry his shoes! He shall baptize you with the Holy Spirit and with fire. He will separate the chaff from the grain, burning the chaff with never-ending fire and storing away the grain.'"

His voice firm at first rose to a crescendo as he spoke. The crowd looked on in awe. Lazarus could hardly believe what he heard. Some of the men John now accused may well have worked at one time in the Temple alongside his father. His dark eyes flashed. He leaped onto a rock with the dexterity of a man practiced in climbing and began to speak from the prophet Isaiah. "God has removed his protecting care. You run to the armory for your weapons! You inspect the walls of Jerusalem to see what needs repair! You check over the houses and tear some down for stone for fixing walls. Between the city walls, you build a reservoir for water from the lower pool! But all your feverish plans will not avail, for you never ask for help from God, who lets this come upon you. He is the one who planned it long ago. The Lord God called you to repent, to weep and mourn, to shave your heads in sorrow for your sins, and to wear clothes made of sackcloth to show your remorse. But instead, you sing and dance and play, and feast and drink. 'Let us eat and drink, for tomorrow we may die.' But the LORD of hosts revealed Himself to me, surely this iniquity shall not be forgiven you until you die, says the Lord GOD of hosts. He has revealed to me that this sin will never be forgiven you until the day you die."[3] Then, with a loud cry for them all to repent and be baptized, he came down from the rock and twisting his hair into the knot as he had worn it when Lazarus first saw him he waded into waist-deep water to await those who would come.

It seemed to Lazarus almost like Moses coming down from Sinai with the tablets of the Law. It was a call too powerful to ignore. Try as he did, he could not get to the water's edge. Men and women had queued with the help of John's disciples and were now being led into the water, where he quietly spoke to each individual. Then, placing his hand over their noses, he gently lowered them over backward until they were immersed in the water. As these repentant believers came out of the water, Lazarus watched for some outward sign of change. Of course, they were wet and their hair dripped water, but there was more. The eyes of those who passed near Lazarus were changed, softer, more at peace than they had been earlier in the morning.

"Is he the one?" Lazarus asked. "He isn't what I expected the Messiah to be like."

"I don't know," a man standing near him replied. "I am not so well schooled in the Scriptures that I know what exactly to look for. I only know that Isaiah and Ezekiel spoke of the Messiah as one who comes from the family of King David. It is said that John is the son of the priest Zachariah. At least that is what they told me at Qumran."

Lazarus nodded in agreement.

"But I don't know if he is descended from David. He certainly does not have the appearance of a great king, one who could save us from heathen conquest, someone who could drive out the Romans. Where would a man like him find an army? Besides, he doesn't say anything about that. He only talks about sin and the need for us to repent."

"Still, there is something about him. I intend to be baptized." Lazarus continued to press forward toward the river.

Lazarus' traveling companion interjected, "And I as well. I suppose there is a need for many of these people to change their ways. Some have become too greedy. They put comfort before service to God, not to say there is anything wrong with comfort. My own family lives well. My father is a treasurer in the government. We have always been a family of service, but in that service we have been handsomely rewarded."

One of the disciples reached out a hand to indicate that Judas should come with him into the water. It was a gesture that the man had offered to each person as they descended the slippery bank into the river. Lazarus' friend waived the man away, dismissing him. He did not intend the rebuff to be a sign of rudeness but he was, after all, a young and vigorous man. The ritual washing in the river only took a moment.

As Lazarus watched Judas and John, a man behind him placed his hand on Lazarus's shoulder. Lazarus turned to steady the man in case he had lost his balance as they inched forward. When he did, he saw the man had regained his footing for he now stood firmly on both feet. At that moment, a hand from the river reached out and steadied Lazarus as he walked into the water.

Everyone in the crowd had patiently waited to speak privately with John while the religious leaders all stood off to one side, watching. A short time later Lazarus saw the men mount their donkeys. With their servants struggling to keep up on foot, they trotted off in the direction of Jericho. Lazarus was bewildered. He had heard the words of a prophet, possibly the Messiah. They had apparently heard nothing that excited them either for or against the itinerant preacher. If they came looking for heresy, they left believing him to be merely a deranged man who wanted people to get wet. Of course the ritual washing had been ordained by Moses and repeated by David, but what did it really mean? If you got wet and then went back to doing the same conduct as before, nothing changed. That was the problem. That was why John cried out. Nothing ever changed in Israel, at least not for hundreds of years.

Lazarus knew better. This was change. Something was happening in Israel that would change the world, though at that moment he could not guess what it might be. His mind reeled under the impact of the preaching he had heard. John was right. The people spent all their time working at mundane chores. In his case, that meant pruning the olive trees and tending to the crude stone production machinery that pressed the fruit into virgin oil required for both cooking and religious ceremony. Even more than those pursuits, John was right when he called for the nation to repent of its sin. As he walked into the water, Lazarus knew that this would be the beginning of a new life for him. He had tried to keep the commandments of Moses, but he knew that he failed to do so. John had struck deep into his heart and he understood that being baptized by this holy man meant something had to change in his life. Accepting the message preached would change the lives of his sisters. It would change the life of Israel.

As he waded deeper into the water, now above his waist, he saw John relax. His fierce visage softened. The slightest flicker of a smile passed his lips. Lazarus didn't know what to make of it. Was John looking at him or at someone else? He stepped forward holding out his hand to Lazarus and asked, "Do you repent of your sin? Do you acknowledge this washing as a renewal of your spirit, a clean spirit you will honor and dedicate to the glory of God?"

"Yes," Lazarus answered, choked with emotion.

Taking his hand as Lazarus had observed before and turning him sideways, he tilted him backward into the water. As he did so, Lazarus felt his feet rise off the bottom of the river, suspending him in neither earth nor heaven. He floated somewhere, just for an instance, in a place where he relied totally on the goodness of this godly man to support him and draw him back to a solid foundation. He gagged as he surfaced. Water had gone down his nose, and he now coughed and choked.

"You are all right," John said. "What is your name?"

"Lazarus. I am an olive grower and merchant from Bethany near Jerusalem. I was on my way from there to the colony of the Essenes when I heard that you were preaching here."

"A name I shall remember. Unless I am mistaken you have important work to do for the kingdom that now comes." With that comment, John looked toward the next person in line. His gentle push helped Lazarus start wading toward the riverbank. As he approached the edge of the water, John called out, "Come to me near Qumran during the month of Kislev. I have work for you. You know the way to Qumran."

Lazarus nodded indicating he knew the way, bewildered by the summons coming from a man who did not know him. He took a hesitant step before looking back. John's expression gave away nothing. He seemed to be looking past Lazarus now to the man who had stood on the riverbank.

Judas had waited at the edge of the river during this conversation. "What did he say to you? He said nothing to me after I was washed." Judas commented.

"He told me to come to him during the month of Kislev and help him in his ministry. What do you make of that?"

The man frowned. "Only that he didn't want my help. Perhaps I am not good enough." Whether he said this out of conviction or jealousy that John had not chosen him, Lazarus never knew.

"I don't believe that. In the eyes of God we are all sinners. No one is more worthy than others. I told him where I lived. Possibly it is because I am within a one-day walk of Qumran that he asked me."

Judas appeared disappointed. "All I can say is that he isn't the One. I expected something more than a wild man in the wilderness to be the Messiah. Sure, I was moved by his words and want to believe in the need for Israel to repent of its sin, but now that I've been washed and had a few minutes to think it over, I doubt much will happen as a result of John's preaching."

While this conversation took place, Lazarus also heard the voices of and the man who had followed him into the river. Suddenly he heard a noise, a voice perhaps, that he could not identify. He turned to face the man John had just baptized as he came out of the water. Their eyes met and for an instant Lazarus thought the man would speak. He did not. His gaze turned instead to Judas, whom he seemed to acknowledge, staring directly into his eyes. He then walked by in the direction of the wilderness.

"What now?" Lazarus asked. "We came here to see and hear John preach. I suppose there is nothing more for me to do but return to Bethany and tell my sisters what I have seen and heard."

"Just so," Judas answered. "I should return to my father's

house. But first I will stop at Gerasa. Do you know it?"

"Only what I've heard. It is far away from my home. They say it is an important Roman city filled with pagan temples and riotous living. Why do you want to go there?"

"For just that reason it is on my way to Gamala. I want to see for myself. Surely going can't be wrong. I only want to see and then will go on home. I hope to meet you again one day. You have been a good traveling companion. Shalom aleichem."

"I desire that also. Aleichem shalom."

The men clasped hands then Judas turned and walked away disappearing into the flood-ravaged riverbank. Lazarus watched as he was enveloped by the crooked path that led into the deep ravines. He then turned and walked with a renewed spirit back toward Jericho and the road that would take him home.

Lazarus hurried back toward Bethany but exercised caution constantly on the lookout for trouble. He had much to relate to Mary and Martha. He did not understand all that he had seen and heard but hoped that those wise women could help him. He reached Jericho on the third day and realizing it would not be safe to undertake the rigorous climb late in the day retraced his steps to the inn where he had shared a room with Judas nearly a week earlier. He liked the man, yet there was something about him that disturbed

Lazarus. Outwardly, he seemed to be a man sharing the same aspirations as Lazarus to live a godly life. But he had far too much interest in worldly matters. The business about stopping at Gerasa bothered Lazarus. It was not on the way to Gamala. It was southeast of where they had stood not northeast. They had not been far south of the confluence of the Yarmuk and Jordan rivers at the time. Why had he not just followed the Yarmuk River valley to his home?

Gamala represented stability, Gerasa the opposite. He had heard nothing good about the place. Would that place have too great an influence on his new friend? Gerasa was said to be a city of over a hundred thousand people, a city the size of Rome itself, with ten major squares. Temples with pillared buildings and broad cardos, avenues where great parades and spectacles were held, radiated out from each square. It was said to be a place of gambling, prostitution, lavish public baths, and pagan worship. Why would Judas want to have anything to do with such a place? Wine and revelry had brought many a good Jewish boy to his ruin in just such a place. Wasn't it that kind of living that led Samson to his ruin: riotous living and a sensual woman? Judas had shown more interest in these things than Lazarus thought healthy. He also had money, much more money than Lazarus. He seemed fascinated by power and wealth even though he did not appear to approve of the scribes who accompanied the Pharisees and Sadducees to the river.

Lazarus pitied his friend. The man searched with such sincerity yet he allowed doubt or rejection to disappoint him.

As he drifted off to sleep, his mind turned to the events of his own baptism and what he saw and heard immediately following while he had talked with Judas. He wanted to share that experience with his sisters. Yes. Tomorrow evening he would be home and could tell them all about it.

Chapter 5

Lazarus left early the following morning for the difficult climb up the mountain to his home after spending the last of his money on lodging and breakfast. The thought of reaching his home and the company of Mary and Martha comforted him. The journey had been an exciting experience but the anticipation of being home sent a dull ache of longing through his body. As he climbed he thought about all the things he could tell them. First, the trip down to Jericho with the merchant, and then stumbling onto Judas and the interesting conversations they had. He wanted them to know the thrill he had hearing John preach and the strange occurrence at the riverbank following his baptism. What would his sisters make of it?

Just as he anticipated, the trip up from the rift took a tremendous toll on him. He traveled alone on the ascent knowing others who could not match his progress might delay him. The pace he set, partly out of anticipation and partly out of anxiety, stressed his body to the point of near exhaustion. The headache and fatigue increased as he climbed. He had suffered from headaches most of his adult life but lately he noticed that they were different. His sisters were the only ones who knew. He told them that the attacks felt like pressure increased in his skull and his neck stiffened on the left side. He said that he believed the attacks were caused by work in the olive grove, looking up while he pruned the trees. He knew better so did they. The truly severe attacks had begun shortly after his thirtieth birthday and were now increasing in frequency. He stopped to rest on the ascent when he could go no further and then only for a short. He longed to be home with Mary and Martha. They would apply oil to his temples and eyelids. That always seemed to help.

The sun hung low on the horizon by the time he walked through Bethany and slowly trudged up the low hill that stood between the huts in the village and his large house near the top. The hours of daylight were short at this time of year. He was glad to be at the end of his journey while the sun still provided light. It gratified him to see Mary and Martha sitting on a bench near the door watching for his return.

They leaped to their feet when they saw his dusty and tired body approaching. He no longer walked with the vigorous step of the young man who had departed. His gait now had the appearance of an old man who labored to walk upright and in a straight line. As he drew closer he knew they could see the strain in his eyes as he squinted against the pain in his head.

They met not more than a hundred feet from the house where they exchanged hugs.

"Did you find John?" Mary asked.

"Where did you go?" Martha chimed in.

Then the questions came like dust storms on the desert.

"What did you see?"

"What did you do?"

"Were there many people there?"

"Is he the One? Is he the Messiah?"

"Wait. Wait. Please give me a chance," Lazarus answered. "I will tell you all about it, but first I must rest and put oil on my temples and eyelids. I am suffering from a headache."

"Of course you are," Mary answered. "We could tell from the way you walked and held your head that you were hurting. I am sorry that we questioned you without giving you a chance to rest."

"No. I want to tell you all about it. It was a wondrous experience. I only wish you had been there with me. But please get the oil and I will begin in a few minutes."

The women entered the house while Lazarus sat on the bench and unfastened his sandals. He unloosed the braid in his hair, thinking: Possibly I have just pulled it too tight. But he knew better. He poured water into the bowl and washed his face, arms, and hands. Hair pulled into a tight braid had nothing to do with the way he felt. Rest and the oil would have to cure him.

When he was once more seated on the bench, Martha took the bowl of water and finished washing him. The cool water instantly refreshed the tired, dirty, and calloused feet. Finally, Martha applied the soothing oil to his temples and forehead and told him to recline on a bench. Mary brought wine and goat cheese from the house. The two women then sat at his feet waiting for him to begin. They did not pressure him for details now. The happiness they felt in having him home safe overwhelmed them. The minutes passed as their brother lay back on the bench with his head in his hands, slowly massaging his temples. Slowly his breathing became less anxious. The tension in his body released. Sitting up, he began.

"The trip down to Jericho was not without peril. There were frightening places along the way. Even so, it went well. I fell in with a merchant and traveled most of the way with his caravan. (He omitted the part about the boy and donkey falling over the side of a cliff.) Then I met up with an interesting man who was also searching for John. He had traveled a much greater distance than I to find him. In fact, he had come all the way from near Damascus to Qumran in search of information. At Qumran, he talked with some of the Essenes. They verified John had been a member of the sect. They said he left suddenly setting out on his own to preach a message he told them he had received directly from God. I think some of them thought he was a little crazy. After all, God has not spoken to anyone in over 300 years. At least that is what Judas Iscariot told me."

The man's name meant nothing to either woman at the time. "Yes and then what happened?" Mary wanted to know.

"It was late in the day, so we spent the night in Jericho

and got an early start the next morning. Two days later, we found John just where the Essenes said we would. Apparently, he had told them where he intended to go. Anyway, we got to a place on the Jordan River late in the evening just as he was leaving. I saw him walk into the hills beyond the river valley. We did not follow him. A great crowd had gathered possibly as many as five hundred men and women, even a few children. A camp had been established, and even though no one knew anyone else, we all shared what little we had. It proved to be an experience unlike anything I've known before. There were religious leaders there as well. I recognized members of the Pharisees and the sect of the Sadducees and some scribes from the temple in Jerusalem. At first we were comforted by their presence and expected that they would celebrate the experience with us."

"I take it from your comment they did not." Martha had picked up on the difference between expectation and fulfillment when it came to the religious leaders of their day.

"You are right. Someone in the crowd approached one of them and greeted him as we always do. He did not return the greeting but turned away and got on his animal. He just left us all standing there. We could see a village about a Sabbath day's walk to the north. He and his companions rode away toward the houses. We watched them as they went the whole way. I am certain that if one of us had tried to accompany them they would have had something to say about it.

"Anyway, we made the most of it. We did our best to observe the Law Moses gave us as well as the restrictions the leaders have added. They returned the following morning just as John walked back down to the river. The contrast was striking. I could tell that John and they were enemies. In fact, at one point, he looked directly at them and said, let me try to recall the exact words. It was something like this, 'You sons of snakes! Who said that you could escape the coming wrath of God? Before being baptized, prove that you have turned from sin by doing worthy deeds. Don't try to get by as you are, thinking: We are safe for we are Jews—descendants of Abraham.'"

"What did they say to that?" Martha asked.

"Nothing; they didn't say anything. He just continued preaching. 'What should we do then?' the crowd asked. He answered, 'The man with two tunics should share with him who has none, and the one who has food should do the same.' It was just what we had done the night before. We knew he wasn't talking to us. He was talking to the hypocrites he said were undermining our faith. Then he went on in reply to some tax collectors who came to be baptized. They asked him what they should do and he told them to stop collecting more than was required. When some soldiers questioned him he told them to stop extorting money from the people. He said everyone knew they accused people falsely so they could increase their own wealth. He told them God knew everything.

"Yes, yes, yes, but is he the One, the Messiah?" Martha pressed him.

"I don't think so, but I cannot be certain. He preaches a powerful message and baptizes everyone who will repent of their sins. I was so moved by his preaching that I was baptized. In fact, he asked me to come to him during the month of Kislev. He will be near Qumran on the Dead Sea. I suppose it will be warmer there during the winter months."

"Wonderful! So you are to become a disciple." Mary could hardly restrain herself. "But why must you wait so long?" The words had no more passed her lips than she frowned. She had apparently just then realized what his absence would mean for them and the olive trees. Who would tend the trees and press the fruit?

"I don't know. He seems to know so much. Possibly he knew that I would have much to do during the summer. But there is more. As I was coming out of the river, another man walked out to meet him. Then he said something I did not hear. John said, 'I need to be baptized by you, and do you come to me?' The man answered him, but I couldn't hear what he said. He was a soft-spoken man. Then John baptized him."

Mary asked, "What do you think that was all about?"

"I don't know. I am nearly certain John is not the Messiah but he says things that make me question whether he is just being modest. If so, it would not seem to be his nature. Anyone who will take on the religious leaders as I've just told you is certainly not timid. He is straightforward and honest. Anyway, there is more. While I stood talking to Judas with my back to the river, the man came out of the water. I heard something but can't be sure what it was. It sounded a little like the rustling of leaves in the wind or the rushing of water. Of course, we were standing beside the river, but we were in an eddy where there was no running water. It almost sounded like someone said something. I think John and the man both heard it, but they did not answer or say anything."

Martha responded, "This is very strange."

Lazarus continued. "It certainly is, but when the man came out of the river, he passed right by me. He looked me in the eye. I've never experienced anything like it. His eyes were soft but penetrating. He seemed to know me. At least he seemed to acknowledge me as a friend and then he looked at the man with me. His countenance changed. I don't know what it was but he looked sad. Then he just walked on by."

Mary rose from where she sat and approached her brother. Leaning over she kissed him lightly on the forehead and stroked his hair. He looked up into her eyes but said nothing. He took her hand and pressed it to his lips. Fatigue from his week-long ordeal overcame him and he once again leaned back wanting to show Martha his love as well, but Martha was intrigued by what he had said and pressed on.

"What did he look like, the man?"

Mary peered into the cup before Lazarus and seeing it was empty carried it across the room to refill it with cool water from the clay jug on the table. When she returned Lazarus took it from her. After taking a long drink he answered Martha.

"Like anyone else. There was nothing about him that made you think anything different about him than anyone else." He stopped for a second before adding. "The only thing that set him apart was his eyes. Someone said he was a carpenter. Someone else said he was from Nazareth. Like all of us he had walked down to hear John preach."

"Did you talk to him?" Mary wanted to know as she returned to her seat.

"No. He just walked by me and went on his way. He was alone so far as I know. I guess he did what he came to do and went home."

Night had now fallen, and there was a chill in the air. Lazarus said, "My headache is better. I think I would like to go to bed now."

The two women stayed up late after he retired for the night, talking about what he had told them. Both women were glad to have their brother home, but they both wondered what John wanted their brother to do. It worried them. Lazarus was not well and he appeared to be about to suffer another attack. What would happen to them if he went with John for an extended time? There were so many questions, so few answers.

Chapter 6

Mary and Martha rose from their beds on the second floor ready to face the new day. On alternate days during their brother's absence they had taken turns walking down the hill to draw water from the well. Mary looked for the smaller of the two clay jugs. She would gladly make two trips in order to avoid the heavy load that weighed her down when she carried the jug Lazarus had carried up the hill the day he left on his journey to find John.

When she finished her task Lazarus overheard Martha say. "Maybe we should see if Lazarus is all right. He was ill when he arrived home, and the excitement of telling his story seemed to wear him out." Lazarus did not move from his bed. He had slept well, but the events of the preceding week continued to occupy his mind.

"I'm certain he will be fine," Mary answered. "It was a long trip. He must have walked at least a hundred and fifty miles." Hearing her say that Lazarus smiled inwardly, Mary had no idea how far that would be. She had never traveled more than twenty miles from the childhood home she now shared with her sister and brother. Even when she had married, she and her husband had resided in the next town, only a few miles away.

"I am going to check on him anyway. He is normally an early riser. If he were feeling well I am certain he would be up. He has to hear us." With that, Martha walked toward her brother's room.

Lazarus spoke. "I heard the two of you talking. I am fine. The journey and the difficult climb up from Jericho tired me more than I thought it would. It is a long, hard, dry climb with few places to rest. But now there is much work to do. I will be down in a minute."

Martha quickly retraced her steps and, with a light tone in her voice, called out to Mary. "It is just as you said. He is awake and will be down soon."

Lazarus did not move from his bed. He thought about John. John had not been what he expected. But if he was not the promised Messiah then who could that person be? John certainly seemed to know a great amount of Scripture, but not just Scripture. He seemed to know about people as well. He had known Lazarus was a man with obligations during the spring and summer growing seasons. John wanted him to join in his ministry and could have asked that he do so immediately. Lazarus would have done so even if it meant leaving home and his sisters. In his mind's eye he could see them scrambling to find workers for the olive grove and press, trying to understand how he could abandon them so suddenly.

Ah yes, the olive grove. Now that he had returned, he would have to go down to the village and hire workers. At least his sisters would be spared that problem. He would do it. Much needed to be done. Trees needed to be pruned. A tree more than twenty feet high had little value. Who could harvest fruit from a thirty-foot-tall tree? Old trees had to be removed and new trees propagated from the wood of older trees.

He knew the cycle well. His family had been following the pattern for generations, for centuries really. They had returned to their ancestral land following the forced seventy-year exile in Babylon. The story had been passed down from father to son, each generation describing in detail the location of their home. Each hoped that they would one day return to claim what had been lost when God rejected not only the king of Judah but the people as well. A few had been allowed to survive as slaves and servants of foreign masters. Others were killed by the conquerors. Only common people had been allowed to remain so that their bloodline could be corrupted by the people the conquerors resettled there.

Lazarus recalled how his family had returned from the exile with Nehemiah to work on rebuilding the walls of the city of David, or at least it was the story he had been told. He had been told how these half caste Hebrew Samaritans had tried to stop the rebuilding of the walls but had failed. He had been told how, once the restoration had been accomplished, his family had returned to this hill and resumed their ancient calling. They resumed their business growing olives for the precious oil that would be extracted. His own father had laughed when he told him how, after seventy years, all the returning exiles knew about the business was what they had heard at the feet of their fathers, men who had never actually grown olives. It had taken over a hundred years for the family to become proficient in the business once more. Now, the house of Lazarus, founded all those centuries ago, had a reputation for the finest oil. He did not know how long he had lain lost in thought when he heard Martha calling. "Lazarus, are you going to stay up there all day? There is work to be done."

"I am coming," he called back. He dressed quickly and ran down the steps to the central courtyard. He washed and entered the ground-floor room where he found a meal laid out. The three people bowed their heads and gave thanks for all they had received. No words were spoken since they did not know how to talk to God or for that matter whether it was presumptuous of them to do so. But somehow they knew that they should thank God for the provision of food. Following the prayer, they ate. While the two sisters put away the bowls and cups Lazarus set off on foot for the village where he hoped to find workers.

Word of Lazarus' return the night before had spread throughout the town so several men now waited in the small market area near the well to see if he would be hiring. They were all men he had employed before and he knew them to be industrious laborers. They crowded around him as he approached asking about his trip to find John. He answered each question not hurrying or ignoring any of them. When he had finished, he told them that he had been called by John to join him in the month of Kislev.

One man who had worked for both Lazarus and his father asked, "What does that mean? Who will tend your trees and press if you are going to follow John?"

"I am glad you asked," Lazarus replied. "It is my intention to allow the men of this village to work with me this season. At the end I will select the one who shows the most ability to work with his fellow workers and to discharge the duties I give him. I will appoint that man to act as steward during my absence."

Each man looked at his neighbor filled with hope. Lazarus continued. "In making my selection, I will employ you all at one time or another and assign duties to you, sometimes important, other times less important. In that way I can judge your fitness to act as steward."

His listeners stood mute. After a few moments passed, the murmuring started.

"Pick me."

And another called out, "Pick me."

Yet another said, "Lazarus, you know me. I am a good worker and trustworthy."

Lazarus smiled at them. "I told you I will give each of you a fair opportunity. Today I will begin by choosing

Eliazar."

In doing so, he selected a man who had not spoken the words of ambition. For that reason alone Lazarus chose him first. Eliazar was a man of proven ability not much older than himself who had worked for both his father and him. Then, to the surprise of all, he said, "Eliazar, I want you to choose two more men who will work with us today. I also want you to pick one man who will work alone in the small vineyard with my sisters."

The family friend stood half a head taller than Lazarus and outweighed him by at least thirty pounds. Eliazar had been more like an older brother watching over the younger Lazarus and keeping him out of trouble children frequently found. When Lazarus' father died it was to his balding friend he turned for solace. Eliazar, although only five years his senior, had proved to be almost a father as Lazarus worked his way through his grief and assumed the mantle of head of the family. Now, Lazarus could repay the debt he owed him by giving him the first opportunity at the coveted position.

After Eliazar had made his choices, grumbling once more started among some of the men who had not been chosen. Lazarus took note of these men and heard what they said. During the next few weeks and months each man would receive the promised opportunity. Lazarus did not exclude them for their words spoken in disappointment but watched how each man dealt with the opportunity when it came his turn to lead. That would determine how he would ultimately make his decision. The man Lazarus would name had to follow the instructions he gave before he departed. The man would work but he also wanted one who could take charge, someone the others would obey. The years of working with his father had taught him that disappointment frequently led to opportunity. For others, he knew it worked the other way.

On this first day, the men chosen started the short walk up the hill to the house with the vineyard and olive grove beyond.

"Eliazar," Lazarus confided to the man alone, "you are to be in charge. I mean by that that you are to take complete charge of the work today. Assign work to each man, including me. I will work under your supervision."

Eliazar nodded that he understood. When they reached the courtyard he turned and spoke. "You," he said, speaking to the youngest of the men chosen, "will work with Lazarus. There are two dead trees that need to be replaced. Lazarus will show you the proper way to take a cutting from a healthy tree. If it is done right, new life will spring from the roots of the dead tree."

The young man acknowledged his assignment. "Thank you, Eliazar. I will do as Lazarus instructs me."

Lazarus could not help but be amused at the obvious attempt by the man to be agreeable in his presence. Time and what they said out of his hearing would say much about their ability to lead.

"Good!" Eliazar looked at Lazarus who said nothing.

"And you," he said, turning to face another of the men chosen in the first group. "I want you to cut down the dead tree. Sorry, but it must be done. I will work with you. The tree is old and will be difficult to remove."

Lazarus gave nothing away but secretly delighted in seeing that Eliazar had not given the hardest task to others just so he could escape physical labor. Both tasks, he noted, needed to be accomplished before new fruit could be grown at that location. Still, if Eliazar was to be an effective steward, he would need wisdom to know when to use his head as well as his back. Lazarus would watch for that too.

The oldest man chosen, a man named Simon, waited patiently to see what his job would be. He had been chosen because of his age. Eliazar and Lazarus both knew that the old man needed the employment that would allow him to keep his dignity. Without this provision, the old man would eventually be relegated to begging at the well.

The old man nodded. He understood he had been given the easiest task but one that needed to be done. He was thankful that Eliazar and Lazarus had given him a job that he could accomplish.

"Now let's all go to work. We will take a break when the sun is directly overhead."

Eliazar and the man working with him entered a room

set into the wall surrounding the house. There they retrieved an ax. Lazarus and the young man working with him selected tools necessary for the removal of foot-long strips from young, healthy trees no more than two years old. This wood they cut close to the ground, where they could also remove a portion of the root. When they had done this, they placed the shoot in a large, clay pot filled with a mixture of soil and animal manure. They soaked the potted shoot in water. They then carefully bandaged the wound they had made in the healthy tree to protect it from insects before going to Eliazar for another assignment.

When they arrived they found one of the dead trees on the ground. Both men were covered with sweat and had draped the top of their garments down around their waists, their olive skin glistening in the late-morning sun.

"I am glad to see you two," Eliazar said. "This has proven to be a harder job than either of us bargained for. We have that tree on the ground but we need to cut it into small pieces so it can be used in the fire. I do not want to waste any part of it." The young man stepped forward picked up the ax and began to work with steady powerful strokes removing the branches.

The work continued until the sun stood directly overhead. Then the men stop to rest and eat. At the end of the day Lazarus thanked the men for their work and paid them their wages. Each man received the same amount regardless of the work he had done. He did not believe he had shown any favoritism. Lazarus believed each man had expended the same effort. From the man who had an abundance of strength, great strength had been required. From the old man, who had little strength, less was required. Yet each man had expended proportionately the same amount of what he had to give and more importantly each had done what had been asked of him.

As they were leaving Lazarus told them to pass along the word that he would be at the well the following morning to select more men. And so it was. The summer passed. True to Lazarus's word, each man who faithfully reported to the well for work took his turn at working as steward and laborer. Lazarus noted the attitude of each. Some worked well when they were under supervision but became dictatorial when given the position of authority. Others shrank from authority choosing to always work without responsibility. Only Eliazar worked well in every position given him. Even when he had been given the lowest and hardest task he worked without complaint while many of the men complained to Lazarus about how others behaved. Lazarus took this information into account and because he worked side by side with the men he heard what each man was saying and doing. Most importantly, he noticed the men who treated him as just another worker without regard to his true rank and tried to distribute the workload evenly.

Long before the end of the season Lazarus believed he knew who he would appoint as steward when he left to join John. Nevertheless, he continued to provide all of the men with the opportunity he had promised in the event someone would stand out. There would be work for all but he wanted to be certain he had appointed the right man as his steward when the time came for him to leave.

Throughout the summer months reports about John came from travelers who had seen him and heard him preach. There had been a scuffle between the followers of John and another man preaching. That had been on the bank of the river Jordan. Afterward, John had departed. Now King Herod bore the brunt of his accusations. That did not mean he had lessened his attacks on the corruption at the heart of their religion. He recognized that corruption had spread throughout the nation of Israel. Lazarus reflected that he might have been hasty in his opinion of John. Maybe he was the long-awaited Messiah. By taking on the political leaders of the country it might not be long before he began to move against the Roman occupiers. But other word also reached Lazarus. A man, a carpenter from Nazareth, had been reported to be doing some remarkable things. He wondered if this carpenter could possibly be the same man who had stood behind him in the line of people being baptized by John at the river. If so, who was he, and why did his remarkable work begin now?

Chapter 7

Summer turned to autumn. The trees were now heavy with fruit. Mary and Martha worked with village girls, weaving baskets to be used in gathering the ripe olives. The men cleaned the stone trough through which the cold pressed oil would flow into vessels below. Excitement mounted as they repaired the press that lay outside the enclosure in a separate walled area. It would soon be time to collect the ripe olives. The rhythm of the seasons always built to a climax with the harvest. The men and women who had performed these rituals honored the customs observed by their parents. It was the time for religious feast and sacrifice. The people brought the best of their yield to God. For the men and women who labored all year this would be the fulfillment of the reward God had promised for their work. Few understood the words of the Torah about why they had been given this hard work to perform. Even fewer believed the ancient promises of a Deliverer. Those who did looked in the wrong place and for the wrong kind of person.

Lazarus and Eliazar worked side by side as they examined the simple machinery. Both men knew the importance of picking at the right time. If the olives were too green bitter oil would be produced. If they waited too long the oil would be rancid. They watched the trees daily picking only from those trees that promised the best oil. Years of experience went into this process.

Lazarus employed seasonal workers, men, women, and children. The men shook the heavy branches so that the fruit would fall to the ground. Children scrambled to gather it into baskets. Women carried the baskets to the press. Lazarus and Eliazar inspected what the pickers had brought. The branches and leaves were separated from the fruit before washing to remove any impurities. It was a festive time of the year for them all. Gaiety prevailed. The days grew shorter. The midday temperature was still warm and comfortable. The mornings were cooler and the heat of the day lasted fewer hours.

The fruit went first to the great granite grindstone that rolled round and round crushing the carefully selected olives. When that had been accomplished they were ready for the second phase in the production of oil, pressing. This was the part of being an olive merchant that thrilled Lazarus the most.

Eliazar watched with growing interest as Lazarus sorted through each basket of fruit, picking out the plumpest, perfectly ripened olives. He carried these to a small handheld press. Placing the fruit in the press one olive at a time he carefully squeezed wanting only the first drop of golden liquid to fall into the special ceramic bottle he kept for that purpose. The resultant liquid was the most prized of all. This oil would be used in religious worship. Lazarus would take it to the priests at the temple who accepted only the best quality oil.

Lazarus felt pride in the fact that God had blessed his family. For generations, they had provided the purest oil coveted by these men.

Eliazar knew how Lazarus felt, but he also understood the reality of what would happen. "Why do you waste your time doing that?" He asked. "You know they won't take your oil. Since Caiaphas became high priest they have rejected your oil. They only take oil from those willing to pay a bribe."

"I know. The leaders of our people have become corrupt. Not even the temple is sacred anymore. It is shameful. The office of high priest must now be bought from the Romans. It was bad enough when Annas was high priest, but his son-in-law...words cannot describe how despicable he has become."

Eliazar argued with Lazarus. "Why do you persist in taking only the first drop from the best olives? They only use it during Hanukkah instead of at one of the three festivals prescribed by Moses."

"I hear what you say, but my father did this and his father before him. For generations, my family provided the oil to be burned in the temple lamp to commemorate the victory of the Maccabees over the Greeks. For my family, the festival of lights is only less important than Passover and the Day of Atonement. For us, the festival of lights shows that Yahweh is still with us. I can only hope the members of the Sanhedrin, the good and faithful members of the Pharisees and Sadducees, will set Caiaphas on the right course."

"But they ridicule you when you take the oil to them," Eliazar argued.

"Someday those responsible for this abomination will pay for their arrogance and greed. That day may not come this year, but it will come. In the meantime I will squeeze the oil as we have always done. And when I am finished I will present it to the temple. If they take it, praise God. If not, then my family will burn the oil in our home to celebrate the time of the festival."

Eliazar nodded his head in agreement.

Lazarus could not know what his friend thought, yet in his mind, he wondered if God's punishment was closer at hand than one might imagine. At the last Passover a man from Galilee had run roughshod over the temple merchants driving them away from the holy ground. Everyone knew that he did this because the merchants were thieves, cheating the people who had no choice but to deal with them. The booths of honest merchants were bypassed. Clearly the man, whoever he was, discerned the difference between honest service at the temple and sin. No one had been able to tell him who the man was but it but rumor said the temple leaders were furious. Their dishonest profits had been diminished.

The hours stretched into days as the process of picking, sorting, and pressing the olives proceeded. When the last of the oil had been pressed, Eliazar placed the precious liquid in large vessels used only for this purpose. It would be stored in a cool shaded place for a month. The impurities in the oil would settle, leaving only the pure olive oil then a clear golden color. This oil they would siphon off into small containers for sale to merchants in the city. Before doing so, it was their custom to gather the family and workers, where they would sample the oil in a ritual relating to the health and well-being of each person. Each person took an ounce of the liquid and drank it, giving thanks to God for the harvest and their health.

Only the mash remained. They formed this into small briquettes to be used as fuel for heat in the braziers during the cold mountain months. With each passing day, Lazarus grew more impatient. The month of Kislev two months off beckoned to him with the promise of joining John. Rumors were heard all during the summer. First a preacher in Galilee, a carpenter by trade, was said to have turned water into wine.

Then there were the rumors about John. He had become ever more outspoken against the sin of the royal family, particularly the marriage of the king to his brother's wife. Herod Antipas, Tetrarch of Galilee and Perea, could have married anyone he wanted—any single woman, that is—and John would have said nothing. But instead of choosing an unwed woman, he had coerced his brother into divorcing his wife so he could have her. Now it was even rumored that the king lusted after his own stepdaughter, Salome. The people wondered how long King Herod would put up with talk he considered treason.

The likelihood of John's arrest weighed heavily on Lazarus' mind. It would be one thing to leave his sisters in the care of a steward for a season. It would be quite another to leave them and then be taken prisoner along with John.

The rumors increased as the first of Kislev approached.

John was in hiding!

John had been taken by the king's soldiers!

John was dead!

Lazarus did not know what to believe. He knew only one thing with certainty. John had told him to come at the first of Kislev, and he intended to do just that.

But first he had business to attend to on the Temple Mount. Lazarus felt exhilaration and dread for what he had to do. He took the special flask of oil to the temple and asked to see the man charged with procuring the oil for the Hanukkah lamp.

"Oh, it's you, is it?" The man smiled, not a smile of friendship but one of a cruel joke. "Have you brought your oil?" His eyes flashed at the prospect of extorting money from this religious fool.

"Yes. It is the purest and best oil we have ever produced."

"I'll be the judge of that," the other said. He removed the stopper and placed his finger over the top of the vessel. Extracting a drop of the oil, he placed it on his lips.

Lazarus was shocked. "The oil is not for that purpose. It is for the Hanukkah lamp."

"Really! Well, it isn't going to be used for that purpose unless you are prepared to pay this year." The man's reputation was well known. For years he had accepted bribes from producers of the finest oil, oil never used in religious ritual. After all, why burn the best oil when it could be used at the table of the high priest?

"No. It would be a sin to offer such a gift under those circumstances. I will just take it and go home."

The man saw an opportunity. "Not so fast. Perhaps I spoke too quickly. It is fine oil. Let me take it. I will see what Caiaphas says."

Lazarus knew the man had no intention of taking the oil to Caiaphas. If he didn't have any money, he could hardly take the oil to the high priest. He would just keep the oil for his own table. Pulling the vessel away from the man's grasp, Lazarus said, "No! I am taking it home with me. We will use it for the purpose it was intended." He turned and without another word walked out of the temple grounds, through the Eastern Gate. After crossing the Kiddron ravine he climbed the hill called the Mount of Olives and returned to his home in Bethany.

The warm months of Av, Elul, and Tishri were now only a memory. The calendar had turned to the month of Cheshvan. Subtle changes could be noticed in the weather.

The temperature fell, most noticeably in the night and early morning. The hours of daylight shortened even more and the sky had changed from dark blue to a soft shade that presaged the beginning of the winter months. An overcast gray forced its way over the sun leaving the residents of the house to feel both dread and excitement. In less than four weeks, Lazarus would be leaving home once more in search of John the Baptist. Mary and Martha felt secure in the knowledge that their brother was leaving a good man in charge of the business affairs. Eliazar had shown himself to be a wise and capable administrator. The sisters accepted his family as part of their own, and he had returned the sentiment.

Chapter 8

Three days before he planned to leave a stranger approached the house in the late afternoon. A light mist had been falling since early in the day and the family had retired early to the warmth of the interior. As chance would have it Mary had seen the man walking up the path toward their house when she looked out of the door. She retreated into the room and told Lazarus that a stranger was coming. Lazarus rose at the sound of someone knocking on the door.

"Are you Lazarus?" The man standing in the open doorway was drenched, his woolen garment soaked even though the rain had not been heavy.

"I am, but who are you? I don't recall ever seeing you before."

"Oh, you have, last spring at the river near Beit She'an. I am a disciple of John."

Lazarus looked carefully at the man. "Yes, I do know you. You were at the water's edge, the one who helped those going to be baptized."

"Yes, and I have been sent by him. You have no doubt heard many rumors about him and what may have happened to him."

"I have but had no way to know what to believe."

"Much of what you have heard is no doubt true. Let me put you straight as to the facts. So much has been distorted.

First of all, John is safe, though he may not be for very long. He sent me to find you and bring you to him. He is not at Qumran as he told you he would be." The man said this so that Lazarus would know he had truly come from John since only John and Lazarus knew he had been told to go to Qumran at the first of Kislev.

"Where is he?" Lazarus asked.

"He is on the east side of the Jordan River in Perea. Many of us who are disciples have warned him to leave the area where Herod Antipas rules but he refuses to do so. He sent me to show you the way to where he is staying."

Lazarus's face reflected his relief at the news. "You will stay with us tonight. We can leave in the morning. Come, meet my sisters. They will be glad to hear the news about him."

Lazarus led the man into the large room on the ground floor. A fire of olive briquettes burned in the brazier, casting an eerie yellow glow across the room in the fading light. The two sisters sat near the fire mending torn cloths, doing so more by feel than sight.

"This man has come from John the Baptist," he began and then realizing he had not asked the man's name, asked, "What is your name?"

"I am sorry. In my haste to give you the news I neglected my manners. I am Shimon. I studied and worked with John at Qumran. When he left I followed him. I did not know exactly what was happening, but whatever it was I knew I wanted to be a part of it."

The two women nodded in recognition as Lazarus lit two lamps. Noticing the man's wet clothing, Martha said, "Lazarus, get our guest something dry to wear. We can spread his damp garments here by the fire to dry. But first get water for us to wash the mud from his feet and ankles."

Lazarus's face flushed. Why had he not thought to offer the man this kindness? Recovering quickly, he got a basin of water and a cloth to dry Shimon's feet. When his sisters had finished, he said, "Please come with me. I have dry clothes in my room."

He led the man out of the house and hurried up the steps to the second story, where they entered the room occupied by Lazarus. He opened the hand-carved cedar chest containing his spare clothing. He said, "You say he is safe for now but you also say some of you have been advising him to leave the jurisdiction of Herod Antipas. Do you expect him to be arrested?"

"Most likely; the king's wife Herodias is demanding it. We have asked him to soften his attacks but he seems to be trying to provoke the king. He speaks of a destiny and will not be satisfied until it is accomplished. You heard him preach. He is a prophet from God, and like the prophets of old times he will not be silenced. In fact, he becomes agitated whenever one of us tries to get him to be discreet in his choice of words."

Pulling the clean dry warm garment over his head he continued. "That is much better." Then, gathering the damp robe they went back down the steps to the ground-floor room where they laid the robe near the fire to dry. They then turned their attention to the evening meal that Mary and Martha had laid. As they ate Shimon told them about John's ministry, how he had traveled up and down the valley telling everyone who would listen that the kingdom of God was at hand. Even most of the religious leaders, many whom he attacked with his call for repentance, acknowledged him to be a prophet. They might not like the messenger but deep in their hearts they knew the truth. He might be strange but some of the prophets of old had appeared to be a little strange in their time too?

"Yes, but is he the Messiah the people have been waiting for?" Mary asked.

"He says not but then what true messiah in our history thought he was? Hasn't God always revealed his deliverers after the fact? Didn't the Maccabees deliver the people from the Greeks? Only then did they cleanse the temple. Yet not one of them claimed to be a messiah. John is proclaiming a messiahship that is different. He is less concerned about the Roman occupation than he is about the relationship of the people to God. Even though I am with him every day I don't know that I completely understand what he is talking about.

Every messiah in our history has been a warrior. What John says sounds different but even his closest disciples are uncertain what he means when he talks about the Kingdom of God."

"I am just glad he asked me to become a part of his ministry," Lazarus added. "Roman occupation is bad, but the influence they have had on our faith is even worse." He then related the conversation he had when he took the first fruit of his harvest to the temple to be used in the lamp at Hanukkah.

"That is what John is preaching against. The corruption of the priesthood has become rampant yet all anyone talks about is his opposition to Herod's marriage. His message is personal for each person, their sinfulness, and the need for forgiveness. He says that the great Messiah is coming, is actually here, but he is not the only one preaching about a coming messiah. I cannot help but wonder if it isn't he who is the Messiah and he just doesn't know it. I am certain about one thing though. Whoever the Messiah is, people are looking for the wrong thing to happen."

It had grown late when Lazarus said, "If we are to get an early start we should get some rest. Shimon, we will make a pallet for you here. We hope you will be comfortable."

"You need not worry about that. We are hardened by our customary accommodations."

"And what would that be?" Mary inquired.

Shimon sighed. "Your brother will find out soon enough.

A room with a roof and fire is a luxury for us. Most often we sleep in the open unless we can find a cave or rock ledge to use for cover. And then we have to watch out for—" He stopped before he finished realizing that to say more might unduly worry the women.

The women said nothing, but Lazarus suspected that there was more truth to what the man had left unsaid than what he wanted them to know.

When the first glow of the sun rose in the east the following morning the men set off for Perea. Lazarus traveled with little in the way of baggage. He had the clothes on his back and a change of garment he carried in a goatskin shoulder bag. Other than that all he took with him was a small amount of money to be used by John's community of friends when they arrived at their destination.

The trip down the Jericho road took much less time than it had earlier in the year when Lazarus traveled with the small caravan. There were no frightened boys or colts to slow him this time. Moving light and fast the men arrived at Jericho just before noon. Two hours later they were across the Jordan River walking past the tents of a Bedouin shepherd. The coolness of the mountains was a memory as they continued now in the heat of the day, a full thirty degrees warmer than when they had left. Even this late in the season with winter coming on the rift gave up waves of heat into the air.

Evening found them once more climbing out of the deep gash in the earth toward the mountain ridge and plateau. Once on top, they turned south and followed the old Nabatean caravan route toward Herod's winter palace. There, Shimon said they would find John dogging sin in the person of the king. Late the following day they turned west again and this time followed a narrow road as it once more approached the edge of the ridge. There in the distance they saw the forbidding castle fortification. Standing high on a hill separated from the surrounding ground by steep ravines hundreds of feet deep stood the fortress Machaerus. Its gleaming white stone palace columns appeared all the more pure by the shimmering water of the Dead Sea behind.

It was near this lonely place that Shimon led Lazarus to a cave on the outskirts of Mukawer. There, they found John with four of his disciples. More had wanted to accompany him while he followed Herod to his winter palace but he had warned them. There would not be enough food to sustain so many, yet he had insisted Shimon summon Lazarus for a purpose no one, not even he, appeared to understand.

The village lay within hearing distance of the castle so John made a practice of going to the outskirts of the buildings halfway between them and the castle. From this point he would shout his accusation against Herod and his wife. As he did so, people came out of their homes to watch, listen, and wait. Inside the fortification Herod sent his soldiers to watch from the towers. On occasion he sent them into the crowd to hear close at hand what it was John said and report how the people reacted. Twice a day the ritual of public indictment took place. Between times John talked to his disciples explaining to them the scriptures relating to the coming of the Messiah.

At the end of the second month the ritual stopped. He now went out only early in the evening before Herod and those in the fortress would begin drinking wine. Lazarus noticed that when John did go out to preach, his message had become more strident. It almost seemed as if he was taunting Herod trying to provoke him into action. It only took a few days. Soldiers came from the castle as John preached. He looked triumphant as they led him, without resistance, into the fortification. He did not return.

A week passed. His disciples had no communication from him. Then, on the eighth day, Herod sent his soldiers to find the disciples whom they charged to bring food to the man now kept deep in the recesses of the castle. He could shout his accusations but no one would hear him except for a few inside the fortress walls. The order delivered by the soldiers was simple, "If he is to eat you will have to bring the food. The king has no intention of feeding a man he views as his bitter enemy." A sense of relief mixed with anxiety washed over Lazarus when the others selected him to be the one to deliver food each day. Lazarus thirsted for the knowledge that

John had but at the same time feared for his own safety. He knew that it would not be beyond the evil design of the king to seek out the principal supporters of John and imprison them as well. He could only take comfort in the fact that the group following John had been watched for months and his was a new face, not one likely to be identified as exceptional.

Chapter 9

The days dragged on as weeks turned to months. Lazarus took food to the fortress prison each day. He spent hours during each visit listening to John explain the writings of the prophets. He impressed Lazarus, not because of his great knowledge of Scripture, though that was undeniable, but because of his basic humility. Lazarus now felt certain John was not the Messiah he and his family had been waiting for. He was more likely the one that the prophet Isaiah had told about who would be a voice crying in the wilderness to prepare the people for the coming of that Messiah. Still, Lazarus did not know who that man might be. All that John told him led him to believe that the Messiah, whoever he might be, was already in the world. Lazarus did his best to convey this information to the other disciples; but, discouraged and with little to do, they drifted away one by one. If it had been Herod's plan to isolate John then the plan had worked to perfection. He would soon be alone. Once that happened he could rid himself of the Baptist. He would hold him in the prison until the people forgot him. His voice silenced he could be released and watched to be certain he did not once again gain a following.

Lazarus and Shimon did all they could to see that John got the news of the outside world. While the fortress lay in an isolated place, news came from caravans moving along the

Nabatean road to Petra and from messengers carrying dispatches to and from the king. Even though the latter were supposedly secret communications people talked. The age-old adage that when more than three people knew something it could no longer be kept secret proved to be true. Both Lazarus and Shimon faithfully reported what they heard to John who seemed especially eager for news from Galilee. Emboldened by what he heard, John stepped up his outcry against the king and his wife. Now he only ceased his shouting when his voice became too hoarse to continue. Lazarus wondered if the months of imprisonment had not become more than he could withstand. His coarse appearance of the year before now became more like that of a captive wild animal. Release did not appear to be an option, but then John did not give the impression it was release he wanted.

At last, there were only two disciples left to John, Lazarus, and Shimon. Others came and went but did not stay. On the days when Lazarus and Shimon were the only ones with him they spent the long hours in conversation trying to keep their spirits high. Eventually, their conversation turned to the carpenter Jesus. Rumor said that he had not only turned water into wine but he had miraculously cured a sick man, had walked on water, and had raised a dead girl to life. Could such things be true? When initially told of these events, John had seemed skeptical. But lately, when Lazarus visited him in the dungeon, he had a strange visage, serene, less intense; yet his accusations against the king were not abated.

Lazarus later recalled the day with clarity. It had been on a day following the Sabbath when John said to him, "I must know."

The words surprised Lazarus. He had never heard John speak anything but certitude. Now he questioned. "Know what, Rabbi?"

"For your sake, it is important that you know if the man you continually report about is the Messiah."

Lazarus now understood. "You think this man Jesus is the Messiah?"

"That is what I want you to find out. The Messiah is the deliverer. The name Jesus is derived from the man Moses named as the deliverer, Joshua. But the name Jesus is a common one. There are many men with that name going around the countryside claiming to be the Messiah. It is important that you know if this Jesus is the true Messiah or just another imposter."

"Why now? Why is it so important for us to leave you? There are only the four of us left to help you, and two of them do not stay with you all the time. Who will look after you?"

John answered, "You ask why now. It is because my time is growing short. Herod will not allow me to live much longer."

Lazarus looked upon the man he had once viewed with awe but now called friend. "Well, what we know is that the rumors say someone by that name has been in Galilee, Jerusalem, and Samaria. Is it possible for the Messiah to go to the unbelievers of Samaria?"

"Don't you see that that is what I am saying? Is this one man or several? If it is the same man he most assuredly would go to Samaria even though the religious leaders would condemn him for doing so. There is only one way for you to find out."

"The last report we had was that the man Jesus was in Galilee, somewhere in the region of the Sea of Galilee. He moves around from all the reports and he may have gone on from there by now. After all, that last report will be a month old by the time we can get there. What do you want us to do?"

"You and Shimon will have to go to Galilee and find out. If he has gone on, and if the man you seek is the true Messiah, people will be talking. They will lead you to him."

The expression on Lazarus' face said he did not want to leave. Nevertheless he said. "We can go whenever you say."

"It is important that you leave as soon as possible. Come back when you have an answer. It is important for me to know. You have been faithful to me and I want to know you have found him."

"We will leave at once but first I will bring more food,

enough for you while we are gone."

John shook his head dismissively. "Don't worry about that. I won't need more provisions than God will provide. Go at once."

Lazarus looked with sadness at his friend and mentor. The man no longer had the same fierce look in his eye that Lazarus noticed that day a year earlier at the river. Then he had challenged the religious leaders sending them scurrying back like so many rats to their nest. His eyes now had a sadness that the few people who saw him could not help but recognize. The months in prison had taken their toll. The ferocious expression returned only when he shouted his accusations against the king as representing everything that was wrong with Israel. His hair, once long and flowing had become matted and dirty. His beard had grown long and shaggy, beginning to show streaks of gray.

He reached out and took Lazarus by the shoulder peering into his eyes. "There is more, things you don't know but should. The man who stood behind you in line as you were baptized last year, that man is named Jesus. He is my cousin. His mother not much more than a child when she conceived him is the cousin of my mother. My own mother was thought to be beyond child-bearing age when I was born. I have told you much about the Scriptures relating to the coming of the Messiah. The time I spent copying the writings of the prophet Isaiah while living with the Essenes caused me to focus on the meaning that God himself had revealed to Isaiah. God promised a deliverer and sent me to proclaim the time. Now is that time. The Messiah is in the world, and it is important that He be recognized. It is not enough that I know who He is. He will reveal himself by His words and deeds, but it is for each person, man and woman, to recognize Him." As he spoke his eyes lit with the zeal he felt in his heart. "Remember all that I have taught you so that you will not be misled by false doctrine. Others will attempt to force it on you. It is not just the leaders of our faith who have a perverted notion about our God. There are others who are willing to mix the truth with foreign philosophies and by doing so make up their own religions to their destruction. I know many people believe me to be mad. I have been a voice crying in the wilderness, and soon my voice will be silenced. But my work is finished. I have trained you and Shimon and the others. You know the truth and you know who to look for. I send you with the knowledge that you will find the true Messiah. Now go, and may the peace of our Lord accompany you!"

Turning to leave Lazarus struck his fist against the iron door of the dungeon cell making only a low thud of flesh on the cold, hard rough surface. There was no acknowledgment from the outside. Lazarus considered banging again and shouting, then thought better of the idea. Coming to the prison every day had been a heavy burden, never knowing when Herod or the guard might decide to hold him hostage as well. If they did, who would know or even care? Certainly Shimon would inquire; but what if they said nothing or denied any knowledge of where he had gone? How would his sisters survive over the years without him? He felt dizzy, confused by the combination of stress and the lack of any answers.

He had been admitted by the one-eyed guard, the one with the reputation for violence. The empty socket where the eye had once been was only marginally more evil-looking than the hard, cold stare that came from the other. Not fit for other duty the man had been forced to endure duty in the dungeon, a duty where his penchant for mistreating prisoners could be exercised. Lazarus dreaded the days when he knew the man would be on duty.

Minutes passed, a seeming eternity, before a grunt came from outside the locked door. Lazarus heard the sound of the drunken guard's booted feet scuffling on the limestone slab floor. A minute later he heard the scraping sound of the large key being inserted in the lock and the squawk of iron on iron as the heavy door swung open. A large rat darted into the cell heading toward the bag of food lying on the crude table beside the stone bed carved into the wall of the cell. Along the way the rodent sent the clay drinking bowl crashing to the floor shattering it into pieces. Without looking at either John or the guard, Lazarus hurried out and quickly climbed the rough steps up to the guard barracks above and then out into the fading light of the winter day.

Shimon waited for him in the cave where they had made their home. When he saw his companion going down the far side of the ravine that separated the fortress from the village he added fuel to the fire and placed two small pieces of goat meat on sticks to roast over the open fire. As Lazarus crossed the bottom of the gash, Shimon turned the meat. He waited but could not see the man as he climbed slowly up the precipice. From where the cave opened Shimon could not see the final quarter-mile of the climb. At last he saw him walking with difficulty weaving slightly from side to side the last few steps.

When he reached the opening of the cave, Lazarus called out, "He wants us to go to Galilee and find the man called Jesus. He wants us to find out if the man we have been hearing about is the Messiah. We are to leave at once. Let's eat tonight and leave early at first light."

Shimon did not understand. "What is it you say? Here, have some food and calm down. Then tell me about it."

The long shadows of night now encompassed their world. Only the light of the fire remained to illuminate their shrinking world and provide warmth. The two men ate while Lazarus repeated what he had been told. When they were finished they moved to the back of the cave out of the wind, out of the cold night, where they wrapped their robes around themselves. Before falling asleep Lazarus spoke again, "He said that the man Jesus is his cousin. He said that if the man we are looking for is that man we will know for certain. He wants us to go at once."

"Yes," Shimon answered. "The only way for us to know is to see for ourselves, but what about John? Who will provide him with food when we go?"

"We will have to send the others to do that. We should not be gone more than a few weeks."

A light snow fell outside but little of it reached the earth. The warmth of the ground surrounding the Dead Sea assured the desert area of that. What moisture did settle on the rocky terrain soon evaporated leaving only the cold of night that followed the setting sun. They looked into the darkness beyond the small fire burning at the entrance of the cave but could see nothing, not even the fortress where John was imprisoned.

Chapter 10

Light did not penetrate into the depth of the cave that faced west. The two men suffered on the cold ground as their body warmth radiated into the rock. Except for the fact that they were free to walk outside in the daytime air feeling the sun warm their bodies they suffered the same as John. He languished in the dark with the stench of an isolated cell barely seven feet square. Shimon awoke cold and stiff in the pale morning light. He longed to be warm at home but he had no home except for the cave. Even the Spartan accommodations at Qumran seemed luxurious compared to this. He had followed John for two years. The idea of home and comfort had vanished except in the recess of his mind.

He rolled over shifting his weight from one side to the other so that he could see the opening. The fire had gone out long ago. Only the stale smell of damp sulfur ash remained in the fire pit along with the unburned blackened rock residue that had once held the combustible material. The sun would soon rise in the sky driving away the dampness of the early desert morning then only the offensive odor of rotten eggs would remain.

He looked at his companion. The man did not stir. Odd, he thought. Lazarus seemed so anxious to be on the way last night. Let him sleep. He must be exhausted. The strain of going day after day into the fortress risking his own life to provide comfort for John had taken its toll.

He rose and removed the cold rocks that remained in the fire pit, scooping them out with his hands and throwing them over the side of the ledge into the ravine. He then rekindled the fire. Only a few handful of the combustible shale remained. It would have to suffice. They were not able to carry much at any one time up from the depth of the ravine and if they stayed where they were for long he would have to climb down to the pit by the salt sea and bring up more.

Two hours later when Lazarus had not roused, he squatted beside his friend and gently shook his shoulder. Nothing happened. The man did not stir. "Lazarus," he called as he continued to shake the man by the shoulder. He called his name again shaking him harder. Still nothing happened. Shimon placed his fingers against the man's throat. He felt warm, too warm to be dead. He waited. The minutes passed slowly. At last Lazarus opened one eye. When he did Shimon saw his mouth, the corner sagging with spittle running down his chin.

"Lazarus, are you all right? You have slept too long for us to leave today."

Lazarus tried to speak but emitted only a slurred unintelligible sound.

"Something is wrong my friend. Let me help you up."

He stooped to take hold of Lazarus's shoulders and felt the dead weight of a man who had no strength to help himself. When he released him Lazarus slumped down, curved in a fetal position. Then, slowly he moved one leg until it extended straight before him. An hour later he spoke. "My head aches," he murmured his voice barely audible.

"Praise God," Shimon answered. "You can talk. What is wrong with you? I thought you were going to die."

"I don't know. I feel weak and my vision is blurred. We will have to delay our departure."

Shimon struggled to hear the words spoken softly and indistinctly. "Yes. Yes, we will stay where we are. You are in no condition to leave today, tomorrow maybe."

Reaching for the bag of millet and the cooking pot, Shimon prepared gruel to nourish his friend but Lazarus choked on the hot liquid. At last, his vision cleared along with his ability to speak. "The attacks occur more frequently now," he said. "They also last longer. When they first began I hardly noticed them. Now they leave me weak for days. Is there any more food? I think I can swallow now."

Shimon put the last of the fuel on the fire. "I'll warm it for you. Then I will scavenge for more. We will remain here until you feel strong enough to travel. It is a long trip from here to the Sea of Galilee."

Lazarus lay-back on the rock floor and soon fell asleep. He dreamed of his home and sisters. In his dream he recalled their youth. Their father and mother had loved and provided for them. He saw them all playing games in the olive grove, hiding and seeking when there wasn't work to be done. Their parents were proud of them and had celebrated, it was said, when they finally had a son. How happy they were when he married. How sad they were when his wife and child died. Heartbroken for him they soon followed. He awoke. And even though his speech remained slurred, he told Shimon what he had dreamed.

The men did not leave the next day or the day after that. Each morning Shimon asked his companion how he felt before taking the millet cakes he had baked the night before to the fortress. As he climbed down into the ravine and back up the other side he marveled at how agreeable Lazarus had been in performing this task day after day. Shimon rankled that the guards required this arduous trip when he could much more easily have approached the fortress along the road that followed the narrow ridge separating the town and fortress. The guards required this means of access as a way to further isolate John. The approach across the ravine to the small gate was used for the disposal of refuse and waste, defiling under the Torah. When he neared the far side of the ravine he became anxious filled with the same fear and dread Lazarus experienced when he entered the confines of the fortress prison.

He looked toward the palace. He thought about the royal family. He remembered Salome, the daughter of Herodias. He had caught a glimpse of her months earlier as she flaunted her young sexuality in front of the guards. On that occasion a governess had pulled the girl away from the lustful eyes of the rough men far below her station in life. It confirmed John's attacks. Herod and the people residing in his household are evil and sinful.

Minutes later he delivered the bag of biscuits and departed taking with him instructions from John. "It is imperative that you take Lazarus north as soon as he is able to make the trip. If the man Jesus you are reporting about is my cousin then he will be able to help him. If not, he will die."

"Isn't the man Jesus the same man whose disciples some of your followers argued with months ago by the river?"

"That is the Jesus I am talking about. I have said all that I can about him. You and Lazarus either know what is meant by the Scriptures I have explained or you don't. I can do no more. You will have to find out for yourselves. That is why I am sending you to him. It is for your good, both of you. I know you believe it is for Lazarus' sake that I am sending you, but I tell you it is the same for everyone who will hear his voice and come to him. Don't come here again. It is far more important for you to go to Galilee. Watch Lazarus and when he is strong enough go find the Messiah." John's voice had grown weak. His had lost physical strength from the months in prison. He now cried out infrequently timing his attack for when he felt it would reach the most people. Deep underground and far removed from the palace he had difficulty in knowing when that would be. Only the movement of guards and what little conversation he overheard guided him. Nevertheless the Spirit of God continued to be with him and he unfailingly chose the right moment. As he did so, Herodias' rage grew and Herod weakened.

The days passed slowly while Lazarus regained his strength. His vision cleared on the first day. The following day he could sit upright and stand. By the end of the third day his ability to speak returned to normal. He could walk without staggering although he had to take frequent rest stops. They departed on the fifth day. The night before they left each man gathered what few belongings he had and began packing them in the shoulder bag each would carry. Shimon took care to see that the heaviest items were packed in his bag, one more act of kindness to the man who had become his friend.

They walked out of the cave and into the cold clear air the following morning. They stopped to look across the salty sea and saw the gleaming pillars of Herodium, where Herod the Great lay entombed, a monument to his evil genius and futility. Lazarus commented on the stories about how the murderous ruler had killed his sons and wife. Then not satisfied with the murder of his family whom he believed were plotting his overthrow, he murdered hundreds of innocent babies because of prophesy that the Messiah would be born in Bethlehem. How much like him this Herod, his son, had become—evil, selfish, and grasping at power.

Then they departed. They walked alone with few caravans at this time of year between Petra and the cities farther south going to the populated areas in the north. Every two or three miles Lazarus stopped for rest. He looked exhausted head hanging down eyes averting even Shimon's kindly gaze. He labored for breath during these brief rest periods. His breathing came in deep sighs as he slowly regained the strength to continue. At the end of the first day they assessed their progress and considered it to be no more than fourteen or fifteen miles. Disappointing as it seemed to them at the time, they were that much closer to their destination in the inheritance of Zebulun and Naphtali.

The first night they accepted the hospitality of a Badawī tribesman who permitted them to sleep in the enclosure but not in his spacious tent. Even though the two groups shared a common ancestor in Abraham neither was prepared fully to accept the other. Their bed for the night consisted of what soft material they could assemble on the ground in the protected lee of the large tent. The following morning they shared a simple breakfast provided by their host and went on their way.

Lazarus felt his strength renewed after a night of rest and

food. He walked with more determination holding his head higher, looking forward—but not just physically forward. He looked toward an unseen goal, something more sensed than understood.

Each day their daily progress increased, first by five miles then more. The rest periods became shorter each day with Lazarus rising first and insisting that they press on. They were now well north of Jericho traveling on the east side of the river used by all Jewish travelers between the high lands of the north and Jerusalem. Here, they found small villages of their fellow Jews. Considering the time of day and estimating the distance to the next village they found shelter each night in the hospitality of a fellow countryman.

They walked and talked sharing what they had learned from John. He had told them how to identify the man they sought but the description he provided did not include a physical identity so much as it did the keys to what the man would be like. As to physicality, he told them, "You will find a man much like yourselves. He will not be someone who will stand out in a crowd."

Lazarus tried to recall what the man behind him at the river a year earlier had looked like. If that were the man then John described him accurately. The man he recalled did look just like everyone else. He had been of ordinary height and had no distinguishing feature that made him stand out. The only thing that Lazarus could recall that set him apart was his eyes, his extraordinarily kind soft eyes, a softer shade than the usual dark eyes of the Jewish people.

Shimon could not recall anything about the man. He did recall a man coming to the river and some exchange out of his hearing between his master and the man being baptized, but there was nothing extraordinary in that. It was what happened later that stood out in his memory. After the ceremonial washing there had been the strange incident of the unidentifiable sound—not wind, but he could not otherwise describe it—and a dove hovering over the head of the man as he walked out of the water with his back to John. He swore that John and the man heard and understood the meaning of the sound and dove at the time, but John had not explained anything to him. For the life of him, he could not remember anything about the man other than that.

"That's right. That is the man we are seeking," Lazarus agreed.

Shimon added, "Since we are agreed we don't have a good physical description of the man, how are we supposed to identify him?"

"By his deeds," Lazarus answered. "Surely that is why John spent so much time in explaining the writings of the prophets to us. We will be able to identify him by his deeds."

"That sounds good, but we still don't know where to begin our search. Galilee is a large area and the lake will make it difficult to search. What if we are on one side and he is on the other?"

"That will make it hard but the rest will be easy I should imagine. We will simply go north and begin asking people if they have heard of anyone doing the things we are looking for."

They began to recount what had been told. "The man you are seeking is from the village of Nazareth. He is a carpenter." Well then, that should narrow down their search a little, they agreed, though not much. He would be an ordinary appearing man who worked as a carpenter from Nazareth. What else? Here, their excitement rose. The prophet Isaiah had described him in a way that would make his identification easy. "And when he comes, he will open the eyes of the blind and unstop the ears of the deaf. The lame man will leap up like a deer, and those who could not speak will shout and sing!"

"That will be our way to find him," Lazarus said. "We will start asking for a man, a man named Jesus, from Nazareth, a carpenter, a man who looks and sounds like everyone else, but with one difference. This man can work miracles. Blind men will be made to see, deaf men will hear, and cripples will walk. We will just follow the trail of miracles until we find him."

Having said that, Lazarus thought back to the conversations he had with John concerning the man Jesus. "He is my cousin," he had said. "His mother and my mother were cousins, although we lived in different parts of the country. My mother and father lived in the Judean countryside while Mary, who was much younger, lived with her parents in Nazareth. Both he and I share in a miraculous birth, but his is much the greater. My mother was old, too old to give birth. My father told me an angel came from God and told him that my mother would have a son. Mother told me that when she was in the sixth month of her pregnancy the mother of Jesus came to visit. When she came into my mother's presence I leaped in her womb. It seemed to her at the time that the words of Jeremiah were written concerning me: 'I knew you before you were formed within your mother's womb; before you were born I sanctified you and appointed you as my spokesman to the world.' I saw him each year after we were born during the feasts in Jerusalem. That ended after my twelfth birthday. My father died, and my mother shortly after that. They were both old. It was then that I went to live with the Essenes at Qumran."

"So you did not see him for almost twenty years," Lazarus commented. "I am surprised you recognized him. There is a huge difference in appearance between a boy of twelve and a man of thirty."

"You are right. For my part, I lived and studied with the Essenes until I had my thirtieth year. That was when God spoke to me and I knew what I had to do. I had to tell everyone about the coming of the Messiah. I had to become his spokesman to the world. You cannot imagine my surprise when he came to me at the river, the same time you were there. I had not expected to see him. I had not seen him for eighteen years and yet I had no doubt as to his identity. No more than my mother said I did when I leaped in her womb. Everything I do in life is to prepare the world for his coming. And now that he is working great miracles I am languishing in this prison waiting to be murdered."

When Lazarus tried to argue with John that Herod meant him no permanent harm, the teacher answered, "Don't you see that it is necessary for me to die I must diminish in importance as Jesus begins his ministry, showing why he came into this world?"

After that, Lazarus had stopped pleading for John to take hope.

It was the fifth day of their journey. Shimon and Lazarus walked through the city of Pella Across the river lay the Great Plain of Esdraelon. This was the place Isaiah had described. "Nevertheless, that time of darkness and despair shall not go on forever. Though soon the land of Zebulun and Naphtali will be under God's contempt and judgment, yet in the future these very lands, Galilee and northern Transjordan, where the road leads to the sea, will be filled with glory. The people who walk in darkness shall see a great Light—a Light that will shine on all those who live in the land of the shadow of death."

"Have you heard of a man named Jesus," they repeatedly asked, "a man from Nazareth who is said to be working great miracles?"

"Yes, everyone has heard," the answer came.

Even though all the people they asked seemed to have heard of Jesus no one knew where he could be found. They answered:

"He is an itinerant preacher."

"He is a prophet."

"He has no permanent synagogue."

"He travels all over the area around the lake, sometimes on one side and at other times on the other."

"Go to the Sea of Galilee. No one knows where to find him. He travels so much. He doesn't have a home. He sleeps wherever he is at the end of the day."

"They say that he never goes to the Roman or Greek cities. He only goes to the Jewish settlements. Strange as it may seem, he always walks around Tiberius, never through it."

Another man added, "Follow the crowd. A large number of people follow him everywhere he goes, sometimes as many as two hundred at a time."

Someone else said, "He travels mostly with a group of close followers, sometimes not more than ten other times twenty, even fifty."

"Ask everywhere you go, where he was when they last heard about him."

The last man said. ""What I've heard is that no one knows where he will turn up next but wherever it is miraculous things happen. He heals the sick everywhere. He just appears in the villages all over the region. He preaches and then he leaves. He is a great comfort to all who hear him. He lifts the yoke of sin we all carry. Where can you find him? Who knows? What I can tell you is that when you do you will know it is he."

Crossing the river they came to a lush valley different from the desolation that dominated the lower end of the Jordan River. Everything they heard was true. Jesus had been through the villages. He had healed. He was followed by a great multitude of people though at times he escaped by himself with just a few followers so he could rest. As they walked from village to village the interval between them and the man they sought grew smaller.

"A week."

"Two weeks."

"Which way did he go?"

"Three days, and he went north when he left here."

At the beginning of the third week after leaving they saw an encampment of about fifty men and women. As they drew near, a delegation of four came out to greet them. When they came near enough to be recognized, Lazarus stopped, and his jaw dropped slightly. Shimon reached across to steady his friend, fearing that he was having another attack.

Lazarus touched his hand as if to thank him for the kindness and then said, "It is all right. I know one of the men. It is Judas Iscariot. He was the man with me when we came to John at the Jordan River."

Chapter 11

Judas walked up to the two travelers, his arms down his palms up in greeting. "Lazarus, is it you?"

The gaunt man standing before Judas had suffered much in the last months. His beard had grown longer and he no longer had the well-kept appearance of a prosperous olive grower. His clothes were worn and frayed the fabric torn and dirty. Nevertheless, the long days coming and going to the fortress where John was held captive had been the least of the factors contributing to his changed appearance. The troglodyte existence that hardened many men had weakened his already deteriorating condition.

Lazarus reached out his hand accepting the greeting. "Yes, but have I changed so much?"

Not wanting to be offensive, Judas recovered. "No, I would not say that. It has just been a long time, and we only spent a few days together, memorable though they were."

"Yes and much has happened since then. We are searching for the teacher from Nazareth, the man called Jesus. Do you know where we he is? We were told that we might catch up with him by traveling in this direction."

"Lazarus, you have found him! He is just up the road, on the high ground. I am one of his disciples. There are about fifty of us with him now. He told me that I had been chosen for a special purpose but he did not tell me what." Judas appeared to grow in stature as he spoke these words proud not to be one of many but one of the few.

What Lazarus did not know and could not suspect at the time was that while Judas heard Jesus preach the same words as the others did, his past had warped his understanding. The months spent in the company of Hellenistic Jews at Gerasa had changed not only the man but how he thought, what he believed and how he acted.

"Come. I will take you to him!" Then, for the first time noticing Shimon, he asked, "And who is this traveling with you?"

"This is Shimon. He assisted John at the time of our baptism."

"Welcome, friend," Judas responded. "And how did you come to be in the company of this disreputable fellow," he asked, showing a little of the quick-witted humor that Lazarus had seen as they walked together the year before.

Shimon answered, smiling and accepting the good-natured greeting in the spirit it had been said. "We both serve John who is imprisoned at Herod's winter palace, fortress really, at Machaerus on the other side of the Jordan. He sent us to find your master."

Judas let action be his response. Taking Lazarus by the arm he led them up the gently sloping hill. The two old friends walked side by side anxious to give the news of their activity during the past year.

"I have much to tell you," Lazarus began.

"As do I," Judas answered. "You tell me your news first. Then, when we have time alone, I will relate what I have learned."

Lazarus began by relating how he had been ill upon his return to Bethany following their baptism. He explained how he had patiently worked to find the right steward to care for his olive grove and press. He tried his best to let Judas know how excited his sisters had been at the prospect of his becoming a disciple of John. At the same time he wanted him to know how worried they had been for him because of his failing health and the hardships he would surely face. He then related how Shimon had taken him to Machaerus and how they had suffered through the months of deprivation. He asked how it was that the disciples of Jesus were able to stay with him during the winter months where the nights were much colder than the ones he experienced in the cave above the Dead Sea.

"It has not been easy. We sometimes stay with people in the area where the Master is teaching and preaching, but only when we are a small group. When we are all together as now, we look for places to make camp much as you and I did on the banks of the Jordan last year. Thankfully we have some women with us. They prepare our meals and are a great comfort to us."

"I know what you mean. Shimon and I have been on our

own for the last four months. We haven't starved, but as you can see by our appearance we have not grown fat on our own cooking."

Judas looked at him. "There is more to your appearance than just lack of good cooking. What ails you?"

"I don't know but fear it is serious. I had an attack three weeks ago and have still not fully recovered. Whatever it is, it is much like what happened to my father. He died suddenly following an attack. Like him my episodes grow progressively worse."

"Then we must not tarry. The Master can heal all diseases. Did I tell you that Jesus has chosen me to be one of those who are most closely associated with him? That is why I was sent to greet you." Judas knew that he had already told Lazarus, but he wanted to repeat the words so he could hear them spoken. In the company of Galilean louts he seldom had the opportunity to inflate his ego.

The group walked the final few feet to the outer edge of the encampment. In the center, Lazarus saw a man talking to several men and women near the fire. The man, who barely stood average height, wore rough woven garments. He had the appearance of a tradesman. His hair had been loosed from the braid he wore it in during the hot part of the day and it now flowed freely across his neck onto his shoulders. When he turned to face the new arrivals, his gaze fell directly on Lazarus.

I know that man Lazarus thought looking into the man's eyes. I've seen him before but where? The river—that is where. He was the man standing behind me, the one who steadied himself as we stood on the muddy bank. Those eyes; I will never forget those eyes. He looked directly into my eyes as he came out of the river. He had the same look then that he does now. There is compassion in those eyes, deep caring and a burning desire to do something. Praises God I've found him. I've found Jesus.

"Shalom," Jesus said in greeting. "We welcome you."

"Shalom," Shimon and Lazarus answered. "We have come from John the Baptist to ask, are you the one we are waiting for or shall we keep on looking?"

Jesus told them, "Go back to John and tell him about the miracles you've seen me do—the blind people I've healed, and the lame people now walking without help, and the cured lepers, and the deaf who hear, and the dead restored to life; and tell him about my preaching the Good News to the poor. Then give him this message: 'Blessed are those who don't doubt me.'"

His eyes smiled but his demeanor was otherwise completely serious. Turning to one of the women tending the fire, he said, "Give our friends something to eat. They must be hungry and tired."

Without hesitation the women turned toward the fire. "Come with us," one of them said. "We have food here in the pot."

Shimon looked at Lazarus, his face a picture of puzzlement. "He said to tell John about the miracles we've seen him do. Others tell us about miracles but we haven't seen anything yet. Do you suppose he means to do something as a proof for us?"

The woman nearest them laughed softly. "Oh no; he did not mean that. He does nothing for such a trivial reason. It is just that miracles are performed every day. There is no way we could begin to tell you about all of them. After you are with us for a day or two, you will see what I mean. You will see many miracles before it is time for you to leave."

The two men ate the lentil soup and flatbread and then settled down for conversation with the disciples—Lazarus with his friend Judas Iscariot, and Shimon with a fisherman by the name of Simon. Simon related many of the miracles he had seen. The big fisherman could not restrain himself as he talked. He waved his arms stalking around the campfire. The others sat in amusement at the performance. Only Jesus seemed contemplative, as if to say, "Yes, it is true, but he does not understand."

Judas on the other hand had appeared agitated and spirited Lazarus away for a private talk. When he had drawn the ailing man well outside the circle at the fire, he began. The words that came were not the words of the man Lazarus had known before. The man now talking appeared to be completely transformed. There was an anger seething below the surface, not quite fully out of sight to anyone who cared to look. His inquisitive nature had given way to a spirit of judgment. Where once there had been acceptance, now suspicion, jealousy and anger replaced it. "So much has happened since I last saw you," he began. "I hardly know where to start."

"Well," Lazarus prompted, "why not tell me what happened after we parted at the river?

"After we parted I went to Gerasa, as I said I would. The city is everything we had heard and more. You know that John disappointed me. I had gone in search of him at the insistence of my father. John may be a great teacher but he is certainly no messiah. Gerasa excited me so I decided to stay there and enjoy myself. I had plenty of money and after the months of deprivation I decided a little fun would not hurt me. My father would never know. Besides, the bad news about John could wait. If I had gone straight home my father would only have been disappointed earlier rather than later."

Lazarus listened intently. What was wrong with Judas? They had heard the same words from the mouth of John but had come to totally different conclusions. Of course, John was not the Messiah the nation of Israel had been waiting for. John explained those scriptures to him, *"O crier of good news, shout to Jerusalem from the mountaintops! Shout louder—don't be afraid—tell the cities of Judah, 'Your God is coming!' Yes, the Lord God is coming with mighty power; he will rule with awesome strength. See, his reward is with him, to each as he has done. He will feed his flock like a shepherd; he will carry the lambs in his arms and gently lead the ewes with young."* Those words spoke of John. He was the voice crying in the wilderness. The nation should have been looking for him not because he was the Messiah but because he had to come first, much as a banquet speaker had someone introduce him; so Scripture said the Messiah would be introduced, not in the temple but in the wilderness. As these thoughts raced through Lazarus's mind, he heard his friend continuing.

"As it turned out I can count myself fortunate that I did not go straight home. I stayed at Gerasa for several months, longer than I had planned. There was so much to see and do there. Not only did the city have a Roman government but also Greek philosophers. I spent time listening to them. They are called Gnostics and they seemed to speak directly to me. Like me, they had a thirst for learning, for knowledge and truth. And I had a thirst for other things as well.

"Their words made a great impression on me. I could hardly imagine why the Romans permitted this kind of teaching to go on in their midst. It seemed opposite to the way they live and worship, yet there it was. The Gnostics opened up channels of thought I had never heard before. They provided an explanation of good and evil, why this world is full of violence and cruelty. I listened to them by day and partied by night. But wait. I am getting ahead of my story.

"As I said, I stayed in Gerasa longer than I planned. When I finally did leave, it was not of my own accord. I had spent all the money my father had given me for the trip and had incurred some debts I could not repay. I am ashamed to say that I ran away from those. When I finish telling my story you will understand why.

"I told you that my father had been a man of business in Kerioth. When we moved to Gamala he took a job working for the Roman government there. All went well for several years and we prospered. I thought that all recollection of our past problems in Kerioth were just that—in the past. But I couldn't have been more wrong. When I returned home I discovered to my good fortune that my father had been accused of harboring a Zealot. I know, you ask, 'How is that good fortune?' I will tell you. Had I not found out, I too would have been taken prisoner by the Romans. My father was to be executed the following morning. I fled the very day I returned. I just managed to get away with the help of a family friend.

"Without money and afraid of everyone and everything, I wandered. I had to steal in order to live. Begging was too risky. I know that no one looks into the face of a beggar as they hand him their coins, but what if someone did and I was recognized? I had no choice but to steal. At first, I followed the brigands in Galilee who roam the countryside, but I soon decided that that was too dangerous. Thankfully, I came upon Jesus and he took me in. I became one of his followers, not so much out of any affection in the beginning but because I found protection in the group. It is easy to hide in a crowd. After a while, I reasoned, the Romans would forget all about me. There are so many problems that they cannot be expected to remember everyone. Besides as you can see I have altered my appearance. I am surprised you recognized me."

Lazarus said. "But what about Jesus; you said that in the beginning you followed him out of necessity. Now I detect some loyalty,"

"Yes you do. I am devoted to the man. Don't you see it? He is not really a man at all. He is a god. The things I could tell you about the miracles he has performed. But he confuses me. Just when I believe I understand him he does or says something to undermine my belief."

"Then you believe him to be the Messiah?"

"Of course, though I am not certain what that means."

"Don't the Scriptures tell us?"

"I don't know. They say much but it is hard to understand. I believe that our people have been misled for generations. Besides, there is much to what the Gnostics teach and believe. My understanding of Scripture after listening to the Gnostics gives me a greater appreciation of some of our ancient texts. After all, what can we expect from what people wrote centuries ago without someone to explain them? That was a different time. We need someone to make them relevant for our world today. You surely see the problem."

Lazarus did not. John the Baptist was that very person and Judas refused to listen. He answered, "But what about Jesus; have you seen his miracles?"

"Yes. The miracles are all true. Stay with us and you will see. They are revealed every day. What I have seen in a year following him could not be contained in all the world's scrolls. The miracles occur whenever he is in the presence of people. You will see."

Lazarus recognized the conflict within Judas. On the one hand he spoke of Jesus with passion and excitement. On the other hand he seemed to have some warped understanding of Scripture. His faith, the belief he shared with all his people, had somehow become altered by his stay in Gerasa. Lazarus did not believe that the alteration would be for the best—at least not for Judas.

Chapter 12

The sun set with rich colors streaking across the sky, an artist's pallet in the heavens. Night followed dark and cold. A blanket of clouds partially obscured the starry creation that had earlier been set ablaze. The men and women huddled together around the campsite fires before dispersing to sleep in small clusters. Wives slept next to their husbands. Single women gathered nearby for safety from marauders roaming the countryside preying on the rich and weak alike. For that reason it had been said. "Can anything good come from Galilee?"

People came throughout the night some building their own fires while others bedded down outside of those who arrived earlier. When dawn finally broke clear and cold the small encampment had swollen to over a hundred. Jesus led them along the Sea of Galilee shoreline as people from the surrounding towns joined them. He walked until he found a natural amphitheater where his voice would carry to those farthest away. There at mid-morning beside the water he began to teach them. He began by giving nine examples of what would be required for a person to receive God's blessing.

Then, anticipating the questions that some would have, he said, *"Do not think that I have come to abolish the Law or the Prophets; I have not come to abolish them but to fulfill them. For truly I tell you, until heaven and earth disappear, not the smallest letter, not the least stroke of a pen, will by any means disappear from the Law until everything is accomplished. Therefore anyone who sets aside one of the least of these commands and teaches others accordingly will be called least in the kingdom of heaven, but whoever practices and teaches these commands will be called great in the kingdom of heaven. For I tell you that unless your righteousness surpasses that of the Pharisees and the teachers of the law, you will certainly not enter the kingdom of heaven."* He talked for over two hours, explaining to them what the Scriptures really taught about murder, adultery, divorce, taking and giving oaths, revenge, attitude toward enemies, charity, prayer, fasting, wealth, worry, and judging the actions of others. What he taught was hard for many in his audience to hear. The books of sacred writing had been closed centuries earlier, and exposition had replaced the written Torah. The Jews had become accustomed to hearing the Torah expanded by oral teaching. Jesus did the same giving a new interpretation to what the people had been taught earlier by the Pharisees. His teaching, though largely consistent with what they said, went beyond their lessons in both method and substance.

Lazarus and Shimon stood together listening as Jesus talked. Shimon turned to Lazarus and said, "He is the One. He must be. Not even John explained Scripture so clearly. We should return to John and make our report but let's stay a while longer and see what else happens. It has already been a long hard journey and you still do not look well."

"I would like that, but what will we tell him concerning miracles? We haven't seen any. Besides, what will happen to him if we abandon him? I do not believe Herod intends to ever release him from prison."

Shimon responded, "John is well cared for the time being. Look! The crowd is dispersing. They must have come all the way from Capernaum, Chorizan and Bethsaida. Some maybe from even as far away as Tiberias."

When everyone had gone, Jesus sat down by the water. The strain of speaking to such a large group had left his voice hoarse. He spoke, barely a whisper, to those who remained. "There is much to do and little time to accomplish it," he began. "I will rest here for an hour and then we need to be on our way. I want to reach the city of Nain by noon the day after tomorrow."

Five hours of daylight remained when they set out. Only a group of his closest followers remained as they skirted around the western side of the lake walking close by the hills. By evening they arrived at Magdala home of a woman named Mary traveling with them. The next morning they left at first light following the hills until they came to the path that led past the village of Sigoph. There they turned south going around Mt. Tabor and followed the hillside bordering the

Great Plain of Esdraelon. All along the way crowds of people joined them following for a short distance but when they saw that Jesus did not intend to stop most fell away to return home. Lazarus noted that wherever Jesus went news of his presence seemed to go before him and the people, even in these sparsely settled areas, came out to see and hear him.

At last, they saw Nain less than a mile away. Jesus quickened his pace going toward the city gate where they were met by a funeral procession. Men carried a dead man on their shoulders. Jesus looked around and motioned for Lazarus to come closer. Only then did he approach the widow who had lost her only son, the sole hope of comfort in her old age. Jesus stopped and his heart went out to her. He said, "Don't cry." Then touching the funeral bier and he said, "Young man, I say to you arise!" The dead man sat up and began to talk, and Jesus gave him back to his mother.

Lazarus would not have believed what had happened if he had not seen it with his own eyes. He stood with his mouth open. The teenage boy had been dead. Could there be any doubt of that? And yet there he stood. He wanted to say something but words would not come. At last he mumbled, "It is you. At last you have come to save your people."

Jesus did not answer but reached out and placed his hand on the shoulder of his taller friend. The weight of his rough workman's hand felt warm and comforting. Jesus smiled. "You have witnessed a miracle," he said. "Soon, you will witness another even more wonderful miracle but now you have something you must do. Is that not so?"

Lazarus could not explain what had happened. He would later say that when Jesus touched him he felt his old vigor return. "Yes. We need to return to John and tell him what we have seen and heard."

"I know but it was not for his sake he sent you to me but for your own. He knew who I Am. He knew when I came to him at the river. I understand that you need to complete your mission. When you are finished come back to me. I have important work for you."

The kind eyes looked up into the face of Lazarus. The gentle compassion that lived in those eyes gave Lazarus a peace he had never felt before. "I will go now. Where will you be?"

Jesus smiled. "That will not be a problem. You found me easily this time. It will not be difficult to find me again. All you need to do is seek me. I am easy to find for anyone who truly wants to find me. Now go!"

Without further comment, Lazarus walked back through the crowd where he found Shimon standing in amazement.

"What did he say to you?"

"He said that we should go to John and then return to him. He said he had important work for us."

"Are you up to the journey my friend? After all not long ago you were ill."

"I am fine. I feel better now than I have in a long time. Jesus laid his hand on my shoulder just now and when he did I felt my strength return. I am certain I will be all right."

"Then we should go now."

They walked back to the east setting their path for the gap between Mt. Tabor and Mt. Gilboa. After walking only a short distance they looked back for the man they knew with certainty was the long-awaited Messiah but could not pick him out in the crowd. Saddened, but with the knowledge they would see him again soon, they continued toward the city of Sinn-en-Nabra, known to the Greeks as Scythopolis, and the ford at the Jordan river where Lazarus had been baptized the year before. So much had happened to them in such a short time that they knew their lives would never be the same. Lazarus felt more torn than ever. He wanted to complete his mission. He wanted to return to John as he had sworn. He wanted to return to Bethany and tell his sisters that at last he had found the Messiah. He wanted to share with them the wonderful things he had seen. He just finished expressing the desire to return home when the thought of not being with Jesus caused his heart to sink. He loved his sisters but wanted to be with Jesus even more. He wanted to see to hear and to learn. He wanted to find out what the Scriptures meant. They all seemed so obscure. The Torah had never been easy to understand but now he doubted his ability to know the true meaning of what Moses had written without being with Jesus.

Only then would he understand the writings of the prophets that seemed clouded in mystery to say nothing about books of wisdom and poetry. Even Lazarus unschooled in all but the most rudimentary understanding of the Psalms saw much more to the words of David than mere poetry.

The men now walked without rest stops. By early morning of the second day they saw the walls of Sinn-en-Nabra. In the distance they saw two men hurrying toward them dressed in the costume of men from Judah not Galilee. Soon the men were near enough to be identified. They were the disciples who had remained behind at Herod's winter palace to care for John. Recognizing Shimon and Lazarus the two men ran up the road to them.

"What are you doing here?" Shimon challenged. "Why aren't you with John?"

"He is dead," the older man said. "On Herod's birthday he gave a banquet for his high officials and military commanders. The daughter of Herodias danced. She pleased Herod and his dinner guests and the king said to the girl, 'Ask me for anything you want, and I'll give it to you.' And he promised her with an oath, 'Whatever you ask, I will give you, up to half my kingdom.' She asked her mother, 'What shall I ask for?'"

"'The head of John the Baptist,' she answered. At once, the girl hurried in to the king with the request. 'I want you to give me right now the head of John the Baptist on a platter.'

The king was greatly distressed but because of his oaths and his dinner guests he could not refuse her. So he immediately sent an executioner with orders to bring John's head. The man went, beheaded him in the prison, and brought back his head on a platter."

The elation that Lazarus and Shimon had felt for the past few hours came crashing down on them. Jesus could raise a boy from the dead, a boy dead only a few hours, but what about John? The gruesome image of John's severed head on a platter filled their imagination his hair and beard matted with his blood and for what? Had he said anything that was not true? Of course Herod and his household had led a life filled with sin. The men knew their lives were also filled with sin but would they have killed in revenge or worse, for lust? Herod certainly did not kill to keep his incestuous lifestyle a secret. In killing this way he made it public. Everyone in the kingdom would know. John did not say anything that others were not thinking. The circumstances of the deed made it even more horrible. Herod might not be willing to kill for his wife, whom he had stolen from his brother, but this nubile girl—ah, the lust of the eyes and flesh were powerful. He would kill for what he did not possess—yet.

The men stood on that dusty road within sight of the city discussing what they should do next. Lazarus shared the news about the boy at Nain and the fact that Jesus most assuredly was the Messiah. Shimon suggested that since Jesus did not expect Lazarus to return for several weeks. He had time to go to his home in Bethany. Mary and Martha were no doubt worried about him. The trip would take no longer than the one to the eastern shore of the Dead Sea and back.

Lazarus resisted at first, then relented.

The older of the two men they met suggested, "My companion will return with Shimon. They can tell Jesus the news and that you have gone to see your sisters at our urging. He will understand. I will travel with you. It is safer for two to travel together in case of trouble."

Minutes later they parted company, Barak going with Lazarus toward Jerusalem.

Chapter 13

The first signs of early spring welcomed Lazarus as he and Barak walked through Bethany on his way home. They had stopped in Bethany just long enough to discuss their return plans before Lazarus continued up the road his home and sisters. He shuddered as he passed the cemetery where his family buried their dead; his mother and father, his wife and child along with the husbands of his sisters. They too had watched and waited for the Messiah but they would never see him. At least so he thought at the time. Quickening his pace he wondered how much longer he would walk the earth before he joined them. His last attack on the hills above the Dead Sea frightened him. Yet, after Jesus touched him he had felt much better. He had no difficulty in walking the roundabout route to reach home avoiding Samaria and people with whom he had no contact notwithstanding their close proximity to Bethany.

Then he saw it. The house and its enclosure appeared the same as he remembered, better. Eliazar had maintained it better than he had been able. Should anything happen to him before his sisters died he could count on Eliazar to continue as a faithful steward. His heart beat faster as he walked toward the house—not from exertion but anticipation. Then he saw Eliazar. Anxious as he was to see his sisters the sight of Eliazar working with a hoe in his hand thrilled him. He approached the man who had his back turned chopping at the hard rocky ground where vegetables struggled to gain a footing in the thin soil where weeds wanted to grow.

"Eliazar," he called as he came near.

Eliazar turned recognizing the voice of his employer. "Lazarus, so you have returned at last. We thought you had abandoned us." The good humor chiding accompanied a large grin as he reached out his hand in greeting.

"You have done well in my absence. Everything looks better than when I left. How are the olives? Will we have a good crop?"

"The early blossoms promise a good crop. The oil yield should be above average. You have nothing to worry about."

"And my sisters?"

"Your sisters are in good health. They miss you and talk about you all the time."

"We are fortunate to have you. God has blessed us."

Eliazar paused to contemplate his answer. "I believe we have all been blessed. Mary and Martha seem comfortable with my stewardship and I value their friendship as well as their counsel. Now, my friend I must ask, will you be here for the first press? Will you be here to take the oil to the temple or should I?"

Lazarus shook his head. "I don't know. Who can say for certain? It is all a matter of God's will."

Eliazar nodded his agreement and returned to his work

as Lazarus walked toward the house. He had not taken more than a few steps when Martha exited. At first, she appeared startled by a man standing so near her home. Then she cried out, "Mary, come quickly. Lazarus is home."

Lazarus embraced his sister. She pushed him back to arm's length and looked again.

"You have changed. It is not just that your clothes are worn. I might even say tattered and dirty. You look thinner but there is something more. Something has happened."

Lazarus could not contain himself. "I've seen him. I've seen the Messiah. His name is Jesus and he is from the village of Nazareth in Galilee. John sent me to him. He said that it was so he could know that this man Jesus was the Messiah but Jesus said it was for my benefit."

"We've heard of him," Mary said. "They have told the most marvelous stories about him since you left to join John."

"In fact," Martha added, "he walked past our home at the last Passover. Some people pointed him out."

"He did not look anything like what I expected," Mary said. "He did not have a royal bearing. He looked like everyone else. But then why should he be tall and distinguished? After all, in ancient times, didn't God first make Saul our king? He was tall and regal in appearance but he did not prove to be a man worthy of God's trust. When God replaced him with David he chose a short man like the rest of the people. So why shouldn't the Messiah be a common man?" She paused. "When he passed by here he looked over at us almost as if he had something he intended to say or do but he did not speak. He just went on his way. There was something in that look that was not at all common."

Lazarus asked, "Then you saw his eyes? Did you look into his eyes?"

"Yes," the two women answered together. "They were soft and kind, understanding, forgiving." Martha added.

"That is it exactly. You have put your finger on it. All the way here I have been trying to put that look into words." He then stopped, recalling something. "Do you remember last year when I went to the river to see John for the first time?"

"Yes," they answered.

"I saw him then too. He was the man who I told you stood behind me, the one who put his hand on my shoulder before I went into the water. I recognized him at once when I saw him again, when I looked into his eyes."

Mary's countenance fell. "You are going away again aren't you?"

The pitiable look on her face wrenched at his heart. "Yes. He told me to come back to him after I made my report."

"John is dead," Martha said. "Herod had him murdered. There is rumor about it. The story is sickening."

"I know. Two disciples stayed with him when Shimon

and I left to find Jesus. They found us just south of the Sea of Galilee. Shimon went back to tell Jesus I was coming to see you and that I would return as soon as I could."

The sisters pleaded with their eyes. They wanted their brother to stay with them. Yet, they knew his path had been set. They had lost him to a greater love that day when they agreed he should go in search of John. He would only stay for a few weeks. Then he would go north to Galilee, to Jesus and his fate whatever it proved to be.

In the north Jesus had just finished to his closest followers. Of the twelve Judas had been the last. Jesus did not give any explanation of why he chose the ones he did. They seemed to be an unlikely group. Only Judas stood out. Jesus appointed them as teachers and sent them out two at a time to the surrounding towns and villages to preach what they had learned from him. Judas had a sense of relief when Jesus paired him with Simon who had once belonged to the group known as Zealots. At least he would have a companion who would talk to him. He did not like the others and they did not seem to like him.

Just before sending them out, Jesus gave these instructions: *"Don't go to the Gentiles or the Samaritans, but only to the people of Israel—God's lost sheep. Go and announce to them that the Kingdom of Heaven is near. Heal the sick, raise the dead, cure the lepers, and cast out demons.*

Give as freely as you have received!"

His parting words were the ones foremost in Judas' memory: *"Don't imagine that I came to bring peace to the earth! No, I bring a sword."*

There, he had said it. This man Jesus preached not out of love and peace but insurrection. Then he had said, *"I have come to set a man against his father, and a daughter against her mother, and a daughter-in-law against her mother-in-law—man's worst enemies will be right in his own home! If you love your father and mother more than you love me, you are not worthy of being mine; or if you love your son or daughter more than me, you are not worthy of being mine. If you refuse to take up your cross and follow me, you are not worthy of being mine."*

There it was again. Only the Romans force a man to take up a cross before they crucify him. He is talking about rebellion against Rome. *"If you cling to your life, you will lose it; but if you give it up for me, you will save it."*

He is the Messiah, Judas thought. He doesn't speak directly for fear of arousing the suspicion of the Romans. He is sending us out to raise an army of followers, an army he can call upon when the time is ripe. He makes no apology for the fact that some of us will lose our lives in the struggle for national independence. That last comment was clear enough. If we do nothing, our lives are worthless. We are little more than slaves to the Romans. But if we live and fight, even though we die, we will be remembered as martyrs for the sake of Israel. When he mentioned this to Simon as they walked along the dusty road toward the distant village of Simonias, he got a severe rebuke.

"Be quiet, Judas. You do not know what you are saying. We are to do what he says and nothing more. He told us to, 'Heal the sick, raise the dead, cure the lepers, and cast out demons.' What has that go to do with raising an army?"

Judas argued. "He also told us to watch out! 'For you will be in great danger. You will be dragged before the courts, and beaten in the synagogues, and accused before governors and kings of being my followers. This is your opportunity to tell them the Good News. And the Good News must first be made known in every nation before the end-time finally comes. But when you are arrested and stand trial, don't worry about what to say in your defense. Just say what God tells you to. Then you will not be speaking, but the Holy Spirit will.'" He continued his argument. "It sounds to me like he knows there are a great many people who lack the courage to follow him into the fight against Rome. He knows that even within families there will be some who will betray others for the sake of an easy and safe life. Our mission is to find warriors. If you want to do it by indirect means that is fine by me, but I am going to be on the lookout for people who can be called to fight at a moment's notice. You will have to choose one day just who it is you will follow. When that day comes you will have to answer to Jesus."

Simon sighed. "Let's just do what he said and nothing more."

After that neither man said anything more. They walked into the broad plain that opened before them. To their left stood the great hump of Mt. Gilboa, where Saul and his son Jonathan lost their lives defending the nation of Israel against the Philistines. The ruins of Megiddo stood across the valley. Crops grew and in the fertile valley once the inheritance of Naphtali, Issachar, and Zebulun. Turning in a circle before going west they saw the other ten men, traveling in pairs, walking in all points of the compass spreading the words their teacher had given them. Judas felt completely isolated from these men who had no idea what Jesus meant. Not even Simon wanted to talk to him now.

Chapter 14

A month after he arrived home Lazarus announced that he would leave the following morning. Martha, the outspoken practical one, lashed out at him. "It isn't fair. You only just returned after being gone for months. There is so much work to be done. The olives will be ripe soon, and then there will be the pressing. Who will take the oil to the temple?"

Lazarus did his best to comfort her. "Eliazar has taken good care of the olive grove, hasn't he?"

"Yes but it isn't the same. He is not our brother. He is a servant."

"No," he corrected her, "he is not a servant. He is our steward, a man of responsibility and trust. He is capable of doing everything that I would do. He has proven himself. We all have work to do and mine is north in Galilee serving Jesus. It is settled. I will leave in the morning. I sent word for Barak to meet me in the village at dawn."

"But—," she started.

"No more, Martha. This is the way it will be. I will be with Jesus when he comes to Jerusalem for the Passover."

He left the following morning taking only a change of tunic and bedroll. Barak was waiting at the well when he reached the village. At the end of the week they arrived at Galilee and set about looking for the crowds that followed Jesus. Two days later they found him on a hillside near

Bethsaida. He stood in the midst of a crowd of about five thousand people explaining the scriptures. Even as he did this he healed the sick and infirm. Lazarus and Barak looked for someone they knew—Shimon, Peter, Judas—but in the tumult of a tired and hungry crowd, they could not find them.

Pressing forward through the congregation they got close to Jesus just as Philip spoke. "Master what are we going to do there are too many of them. They have not had anything to eat since this morning. For that matter neither have we. There may be trouble if we don't send them away."

Jesus looked at him with sorrow in his eyes. Lazarus heard the softly spoken response. "You are right. There is a great multitude. What do you want me to do? Where can we or they get enough food? Bethsaida is not a large town. What do we have?"

By now the other disciples who had gathered close by began trying to answer the questions put to Philip.

Judas spoke first. "We have some money in our treasury, but it isn't much. If we try to feed this many people it will take all we have. And even then it may not be enough. I doubt we could buy that much in Bethsaida and what we could buy will be overpriced. The demand is great. They can charge whatever they want."

This was not the first time that Judas had shown his unwillingness to share what they had and it angered the others who grumbled both at the lack of food and Judas' stinginess. Peter for once playing the peacemaker, added, "I saw a boy a while ago who had two salted fish."

Andrew chimed in. "If it is the same boy I saw, he also had five barley cakes. Not much for five thousand people."

The others looked at the brothers as if to say, "Have you lost your senses? Five loaves of bread and two small fish are a lunch for one person not dinner for five thousand." They began to grumble again.

Holding up his hand, Jesus said, "It will be enough. Have the boy bring the fish and bread to me."[1] When they had done as he instructed them he continued. "Have them sit down in groups of about fifty each." The disciples did so, and everybody sat down. Taking the five loaves and the two fish he looked up to heaven, gave thanks and broke them. Then he gave them to the disciples to set before the people. They all ate and were satisfied. After that the disciples picked up twelve baskets-full of broken pieces left over from the five loaves and two fish.

Lazarus stood nearby watching the entire episode. It occurred to him that even as Jesus talked to his disciples in such a casual way, questioning them, he was teaching them. If the others had looked into his eyes they would have seen it. Jesus knew about the fish and the barley loaves even before he began questioning them. He asked the question to make them aware how little there was at hand. He intended to show them God's power to use even the smallest gift multiplying it beyond imagination. And then he had prayed, giving thanks for what must have seemed to them to be the most trivial of all meals. Only then had the boy's lunch become a feast for a great crowd.

Seeing that, another thought struck Lazarus. The lessons Jesus taught grew if one looked closely just as the fish and loaves had multiplied. It was just easier to see the fish and the loaves. He marveled at the disciples' lack of understanding. He wondered would he have been able to answer any better if he had been put on the spot by the question. Still, he could not help but be impressed by the faith the disciples had shown by bringing the fish and bread to Jesus. They clearly expected something great to be done even if they did not know exactly what. It was that kind of faith that stirred Lazarus. A warm feeling came over him as he remembered the dead boy at Nain: I would be willing to do anything for Jesus knowing the power he has, even over death itself.

Two months later, Lazarus made his bed near Judas so that the two could talk. Judas had chosen the spot. During the weeks that had passed since the miracle with the fish and loaves they had traveled over the mountains to the infidel cities of Tyre and Sidon on the Mediterranean Sea where Jesus performed many miracles. Now bedded down near Caesarea Philippi at the base of Mt. Hermon out of the hearing of the other eleven close disciples, Judas opened the conversation. "My friend, we haven't had time to talk since you rejoined us. What has been happening with you?"

"Much! There has been so much happening that I have a hard time understanding it all. We have been constantly on the move. Everywhere he goes huge crowds follow. They want to see him perform miracles, to heal them. He fed five thousand people with next to nothing and then just weeks later he fed four thousand more with little more than he had the first time. He made a blind man see. He drove out a demon from a girl and seems to condemn Bethsaida and Chorazin."

Judas answered. "The twelve of us were with him a few days ago and he asked if we knew who he was. What kind of a question is that?"

"What did they say?"

"Nothing at first, 'well then he asked who do the crowds say I am?'"

"Did you answer?"

"No, I didn't say anything, but the others all started giving answers. They replied, 'Some say, John the Baptist; others say Elijah; and still others, Jeremiah or one of the prophets.' 'But what about you?' he asked. 'Who do you say I am?'"

"What did you say?"

"I didn't have a chance to say anything. Simon Peter

answered, 'You are the Christ, the Son of the living God.'"

"And?"

"I'll tell you what. Jesus replied, 'God has blessed you, Simon, son of Jonah for my Father in heaven has personally revealed this to you—this is not from any human source. You are Peter, a stone; and upon this rock I will build my church; and all the powers of hell shall not prevail against it. And I will give you the keys of the Kingdom of Heaven; whatever doors you lock on earth shall be locked in heaven; and whatever doors you open on earth shall be open in heaven!'" Now what is that supposed to mean? Church, what church? There isn't any church that I can see. We don't even have a synagogue to call our own. We just wander around the countryside like a bunch of sheep."

"What happened next?"

"Listen to this. Then he warned his us not to tell anyone that he was the Christ

"You don't believe him?"

"I don't know what to believe. He has been talking about dying. He has also been talking about eating his flesh and drinking his blood."

"I haven't heard that."

"No. He just talks to the twelve of us about it. He hasn't said anything to the rest of you yet, but I have no doubt he will soon. He is talking about it all the time. I don't know what to make of it. It almost sounds like he wants to die." He stopped and contemplated whether he should say more. "I have started keeping a journal of what he says and does. But more importantly, I hope to explain what it all means."

Lazarus appeared shocked as he saw how much Judas had changed in the two years since they met near Jericho. "I know he talks in parables and that makes what he says hard to understand. I think he does that intentionally though. He always says that those who are truly listening will understand and the others would never get it anyway. Are you certain his talk about dying and eating his flesh and drinking his blood isn't just more of the same?"

Judas bridled at what he took as an attack by Lazarus. "What do you mean by insinuating that I don't understand? It may just be that I am the only one who really does understand. That is why I am writing a journal."

Lazarus had not meant to offend his companion and asked in a conciliatory tone, "Are you willing to share your writing?"

Mollified, Judas answered, "I am. I haven't finished it yet but let me tell you what I believe."

"I'm listening." Lazarus propped up on one elbow and looked at the man he felt certain had lost grip on the truth.

"I have combined what he says with what I learned at Gerasa from the Gnostics. His claim to be the Son of God can only make sense if I look at it that way."

"Go on."

The heavens and earth are not what we have been led to believe. The writers of the scriptures got it wrong. The truth was hidden from them by the forces of evil."

"What do you mean?"

"Just this, we are living in an evil world and it was made that way."

Lazarus started to respond but decided to hear the man out. He felt certain that what followed would not make sense to anyone but his misguided companion.

Judas continued. "The god we have all known as Yahweh, the so-called great I Am, is not who we thought he was." Lazarus knew he was in for a far-fetched story. "I am willing to concede that he is the god of creation, but what are we saying when we say that? Is creation good, of course not; the world is an evil place. It is wild and degenerate. The whole of creation is in a state of chaos. Now I ask you, what kind of god would create such a place? Clearly, it is not a god who is up to any good and that is the whole point. The god that we call Yahweh is actually named Saklas. And while he is the god of creation, he is not the god over everything."

Lazarus knew Judas had perverted the truth but he continued listening.

"Saklas was created by the supreme god to be a fool, a god of folly. He did not even create this corrupt world alone. He had the help of Yaldabaoth, a blood-stained god. The two of them made the earth. They not only made the earth, but they also created mankind. They did it as a cruel joke and we are the victims of that joke. The one true god, the god of everything, is a woman. Her name is Barbelo. What Jesus acknowledged when he said he was the Son of God has to be that he is the son of Barbelo."

Lazarus was incredulous. "What makes you think that?"

"Right after Jesus told Peter that his true identity had not been told him by man but came from heaven, he was just ridiculing Peter. He knows what those fools think. He is the son of a god all right, but not the god they think. It was just his way of having a joke at their expense."

Lazarus said nothing. His mind reeled.

"After he said it, he looked right at me. I would swear that he was laughing on the inside. The others don't understand. They fail to recognize just how great the Master truly is. They believe that he is the son of the creator. What folly. Whatever could they be thinking? This world is a place of violence and madness. What could Jesus have to do with the god of this world? Jesus is the son of the most-high god."

Lazarus could no longer stay quiet. "That is crazy talk, Judas. Think about it. It makes no sense for Jesus to call God his Father if he is the son of a female god named Barbelo. Wouldn't he say that he was the son of the Mother?" Lazarus had heard all he wanted about these ravings, but he could not resist the urge to ask one more question. "What is the point of all this then?"

"I'm not certain but whatever it is Jesus can count on me not the others."

Lazarus shook his head in disbelief. What could he say to someone who misunderstood so much? There was one thing he knew. He would have to find a place and a time to talk to Jesus about what he had heard. Somehow, he felt certain that if Jesus were in fact talking to the inner twelve about dying soon, he did not have much time. The thing that troubled him most of all though was the doubt that it caused. Jesus was the Messiah.

Before falling asleep the words he heard from John the Baptist came back to him. They were the words that John had transcribed back at Qumran from the prophet Isaiah: *"In God's eyes he was like a tender green shoot, sprouting from a root in dry and sterile ground. But in our eyes there was no attractiveness at all, nothing to make us want him. We despised him and rejected him—a man of sorrows, acquainted with bitterest grief. We turned our backs on him and looked the other way when he went by. He was despised, and we didn't care. Yet it was our grief he bore, our sorrows that weighed him down. And we thought his troubles were a punishment from God, for his own sins! But he was wounded and bruised for our sins. He was beaten that we might have peace; he was lashed—and we were healed! We—every one of us—have strayed away like sheep! We, who left God's paths to follow our own. Yet God laid on him the guilt and sins of* every one of us! He was oppressed and he was afflicted, yet he never said a word. He was brought as a lamb to the slaughter; and as a sheep before her shearers is dumb, so he stood silent before the ones condemning him. From prison and trial they led him away to his death. But who among the people of that day realized it was their sins that he was dying for—that he was suffering their punishment? He was buried like a criminal, but in a rich man's grave; but he had done no wrong and had never spoken an evil word. But it was the Lord's good plan to bruise him and fill him with grief."

Lazarus thought he understood. Isaiah held the key. But if Jesus died he would lose a friend, the best friend he would ever have. He fell to sleep, dreaming that he stayed with Jesus forever.

Chapter 15

Many of Jesus' most ardent followers did begin turning their backs on him during the weeks that followed. The crowds dwindled as he talked about eating his flesh and drinking his blood. They were incapable of reconciling his talk of dying with what they wanted in the Messiah. They wanted him to lead them in rebellion and could not understand why he would not even talk to them about armed action against their Roman oppressors. After all, hadn't Solomon himself said that there was "a time for everything: a time for loving; a time for hating; a time for war; a time for peace"? He continued to talk about peace and love, not the kind of love that a man has for a woman but the type of love that God has for mankind. It made no sense to them. In turning away the crowd seemed to reason that although he was a wonderful teacher—he was no messiah.

Jesus did not appear surprised by his listeners' lack of understanding when he talked to them about spiritual matters. He knew what they wanted. He understood their frustration. He had spent the first thirty years of his life working as a carpenter with his father Joseph. The hard work and low pay were made nearly unbearable by the oppressive taxes levied by the Romans, the king, and the religious leaders. No matter how much he paid, no matter how hard he worked, there was never quite enough to support his mother and family. Now that he had left home to preach there was even less. They endured even greater hardships while he did not even have a place to call home. He owned nothing, not even a bed.

He nevertheless appeared saddened when the crowds deserted him. They had been so excited when they first heard him preach. They could accept that Jesus preached love instead of hatred, but his own death? Everyone would die eventually but why talk about it as though that was all you intended to do? The people wanted someone who would restore the nation to the glory of David and Solomon, not die a meaningless death.

As the crowds diminished, Lazarus drew closer to the inner circle. The group traveling with Jesus now rarely numbered more than seventy. Even so, there were many mouths to feed; and the treasury never seemed to have enough money to purchase what they needed.

One day, after they had returned to Galilee from the area of Sydon and Tyre Jesus stopped by the side of the Sea of Galilee indicating they would rest for a few days. Peter, his brother Andrew and several of the others who had relatives living nearby made their way to their homes. Lazarus assumed that Jesus would continue on to Capernaum, his adopted home. Instead he looked for a secluded spot where he could rest away from even the small crowds that seemed to tire him. It surprised Lazarus when Jesus asked him to stay. He welcomed the time that he would be able to spend with Jesus and the half dozen others who stayed with him. After the others had gone, Jesus turned to him. "My friend, I am tired and dirty. I need a bath. Come with me into the water and we will bathe."

Lazarus realized that this was his chance to tell Jesus about the conversation he had with Judas. "I would like that," was all he said at the time.

The man who asked him to come to the lake seemed to have shed the spirituality that marked so much of his speech. This was the carpenter from Nazareth, a small, rough-featured man with calloused hands, a short dark beard, and single braid of hair hanging to just below his shoulders. He was hot and tired and in need of a real friend. They moved along the edge of the water to where some trees provided them with privacy. Once there they both stripped off their outer tunics, removed their sandals, and waded out into the lake up to their necks. Using their hands, they began rubbing the sweat from their bodies. "I have wanted to spend some time with you my friend but it seems we have been so busy. This is the first free moment I have had," Jesus said.

"I have wanted to spend time alone with you." Lazarus was uncertain now whether he should bring up the conversation he had with Judas.

Before he could speak further, Jesus continued, "Do you

remember where we met?"

"Of course; it was at the river near Beit She'an, John was baptizing. That was what? Two years ago."

"Yes. I stood behind you in the line going to see John. Did you know that he was my cousin?"

"He told me so just before he sent me to find you."

Jesus said nothing throwing his head back into the water to wash the hair he had loosened from the tight braid. "John and I were close when we were children. Every year at Passover my parents took me to Jerusalem to the temple. I saw John there with his parents. When we were not at the temple we played together up until we were both eleven. His parents were quite old when he was born and they both died that year. They were not there when we went back the year I turned twelve." A wistful expression came across his face. "Everything changed that year. John had gone to live with the Essenes. I missed him.

"I had not seen him again until that day at the river. In a way I was surprised. I felt compelled to go to see John but did not expect to find my cousin. He was the last boy I expected to be a preacher. His father had been a priest but he never seemed interested in following his footsteps." He chuckled. "But then look at me. I went into the family business, in more ways than one." With that, the chuckle became a full, deep throated laugh. "Oh, my friend, there is so much I want to tell you."

Lazarus saw his chance. He did not intend to let the opportunity pass. "I have much I want to discuss with you also." He pressed on knowing that if he did not do so he might never have another chance. "Several weeks ago, just after you fed all those people near Bethsaida, I had a disturbing conversation with Judas."

"Oh yes, Judas." The very mention of his name caused a sadness to descend on Jesus. "He was with you at the river the day we both went to be baptized."

"Yes and I am surprised to find him a part of your inner circle of disciples. He is not to be trusted."

"I know but I can trust him to complete the task I have for him."

"But he told me some things that are really disturbing. He doesn't worship Yahweh—at least so he says."

"I know that too."

"Then why did you choose him to be one of the twelve?"

"For that very reason."

"But why; how did you know that?"

"My friend, there are many things I want to tell you but not today. Let's just enjoy the water and the warm sun." Splashing water on his companion, he continued. "Tell me about growing olives. I am a town boy and never had any experience with the olive business."

Lazarus considered what to say and decided to drop the subject of Judas. Jesus knew, or at least said he knew, all about Judas. For today, he did not want to be a preacher or a prophet or the Son of God. He was the man that everyone thought to be the son of Joseph and he wanted to relax and rest. They waded out of the water and lay on the soft grass letting the warm sun dry them. Lazarus began talking about olives and then heard a soft snoring come from Jesus. Soon, both were sound asleep.

The next four days were among the happiest of Lazarus's life. He and Jesus walked and talked together. As their friendship grew he found Jesus to have a playful nature when at leisure. At times, while they traveled, he seemed to be more than a man. Now that he could relax and rest his humanity stood out for everyone in camp to see. He was tired and needed to rest. He needed a few close friends to share this time of retreat before going on with his ministry.

To the delight of his companions he sometimes removed his outer garment revealing his well-muscled body, wrestling with Lazarus or one of the other men. Lazarus suspected that the short, sinewy, and muscular Jesus did not try very hard. And when they ran foot races they all laughed. Jesus' short legs could not keep pace with his taller companions.

At the end of the week the others returned. Lazarus watched for his friend Shimon to come but after three days realized that he had abandoned them taking the other two disciples of John with him. The talk of death had finally been too much for him.

Jesus noticed his friend's downcast countenance but said nothing his mind set on what he intended to do next. Autumn faded with the approach of winter. He had much to do between then and Passover. At the end of the third day he called the remaining loyal followers together and told them they were going to Perea. They crossed the Jordan River and began the long slow walk southward through the Tetrarchy of Philip and down toward the Decapolis, the ten great independent cities the Greeks and Romans had built on the eastern side of the river. Even though these were pagan cities there were large Jewish populations in each. The people came out in crowds to hear what Jesus had to say and to be healed by him. Now, after nearly three years of ministry, his fame had spread across the entire world once controlled by David and Solomon.

Once again Lazarus could only watch from afar. Not being one of the twelve disciples he seldom had the opportunity to speak privately with Jesus. On the rare occasion when he did, Jesus confided in him that it seemed that all the masses were interested in were the miracles of healing. In an attempt to draw off the earthly desire of the people, he repeated a sermon he had preached in Galilee. *"For I, the Messiah, must suffer much,"* he said, *"and be rejected by the Jewish leaders—the elders, chief priests, and teachers of the Law—and be killed; and three days later I will come back to life again! Anyone who wants to follow me must put aside his own desires and conveniences and carry his cross with him every day and keep close to me! Whoever loses his life for my sake will save it, but whoever insists on keeping his life will lose it; and what profit is there in gaining the whole world when it means forfeiting one's self?*

When I come in glory and in the glory of the Father and the holy angels I will be ashamed of all who are ashamed of me and of my words now. But this is the simple truth—some of you who are standing here right now will not die until you have seen the Kingdom of God."

Each time he gave the crowd this message they abandoned him. Lazarus watched. His eyes saddened. Not even the closest disciples seemed to understand, not that Lazarus did fully. But, unlike them, he took what Jesus said on faith without the personal instruction they received.

Jesus stopped when they reached the outskirts of the city of Gerasa and sent his disciples to the Jewish section to tell the Jews that he was in the area. As with the other places he went, a crowd gathered to hear him speak. Looking directly at Judas, he began. *"A man had two sons. When the younger told his father, 'I want my share of your estate now, instead of waiting until you die!' his father agreed to divide his wealth between his sons. A few days later this younger son packed all his belongings and took a trip to a distant land, and there wasted all his money on parties and prostitutes. About the time his money was gone a great famine swept over the land, and he began to starve. He persuaded a local farmer to hire him to feed his pigs. The boy became so hungry that even the pods he was feeding the swine looked good to him. And no one gave him anything. When he finally came to his senses, he said to himself, 'At home even the hired men have food enough and to spare, and here I am, dying of hunger! I will go home to my father and say, Father, I have sinned against both heaven and you, and am no longer worthy of being called your son. Please take me on as a hired man."*

As the story ended, Jesus said, "Of course, when the boy returned home, his father forgave him for his transgression and restored him to the family."

Lazarus recalled the story Judas had told him about what happened when he stopped at Gerasa three years earlier. He understood that the story Jesus told had a double meaning. Jesus was telling Judas that he knew what had happened there and that it would be forgiven. As bad as it might seem to Judas, it would not be the one thing that would keep him from being accepted by Jesus' Father.

Judas, who stood near Lazarus, looked down at his feet and refused to acknowledge either Lazarus or Jesus. If he understood, he never revealed the fact. As the crowd dispersed Lazarus saw a man standing nearby who appeared to want a conference with either him or Judas. The man moved forward but stopped when he noticed Lazarus. Then turning away he walked back into the city.

Chapter 16

Winter in the mountainous region between the Yarmuk and Jabbok rivers sent a physical and spiritual chill through the men. Jesus felt the chill along with the remaining disciples knowing his time on earth was growing short. He paired them as he had the Twelve a year earlier and sent them to the villages he planned to visit in the spring. Names were called and men given their instructions. As the group remaining dwindled to a handful Lazarus became concerned. He waited for his name to be called believing that even though he was not one of the closest twelve disciples he would now be included in the group of seventy. His hopes dropped as the pairings reached fifty and then sixty. Still, he continued to believe his name would be called even if he were to be number seventy. But when Jesus completed giving his assignments and Lazarus had not heard his name called he could not hide his disappointment.

"Jesus, why didn't you call my name? Haven't I been loyal and faithful to you?"

"Oh, my dear friend," he replied, "you are important to me! Do not think because I did not give you this one thing that I do not value you just as much as all these others. No, it is because I have something even more important for you to do."

Lazarus was not about to be dismissed with such a

general answer. "But if not now, when? You have said that your time is growing short and that you will soon be betrayed. When will I ever have a chance to serve you?"

"Don't let your heart be troubled. You will be evidence my Father's power before spring comes. Will you trust me?"

"You know I will," Lazarus replied. The words came easy but the how, the when, the where puzzled him.

"That is why you were chosen. Much of what the others have heard from me you were told by my cousin John. He taught you from the ancient scriptures of prophecy while I taught those closest to me with new words that I received from the Holy Spirit. Yet you are the one who understands and believes while the others struggle. It is for that reason that I am sending them out with power over demons. They are armed with the power to heal and preach. They have known hardship while traveling with me but I am now sending them out on their own. They will have to trust me as I know you trust me. They will be rejected in many of the places they go because they are coming in my name. Not everyone who hears of me will accept me or my messenger. But if they do not, it will be to their own detriment. Everyone in Israel will have a chance to hear the good news that I Am in the world."

"But what am I supposed to do? When the others leave you and I will be left alone."

"Just so! Hanukkah will soon be celebrated. I want to go

up to Jerusalem while the others are traveling. I want you to go with me. I would like to stay with you and your sisters at Bethany."

His heart now lifted, Lazarus answered, "Wonderful. When do we leave?"

"I want to be certain that the others are off safely and understand what they are to do. We will then go down to the river crossing Joshua used near Jericho." After saying this he gave final instruction to those disciples he had chosen to cross the Jordan River near Aenon and proceed through Samaria.

The following day the last of the seventy disciples departed. Jesus and Lazarus then began the long walk to the river crossing and the high cliff road that led from Jericho to Jerusalem. They covered the distance faster than Lazarus imagined possible but then everything seemed to be possible for Jesus.

Toward the end of the third day they reached the place where the Jericho road began the winding, treacherous ascent. Soon they were in deep shadows reminding Lazarus of the psalm about the valley of the shadow of death, only this was no valley. No matter how many times he climbed or descended this road it always frightened him.

Jesus knowing the fear in his heart spoke words of reassurance. "On the way here you asked me how I knew that Judas would betray me. I did not answer then but I will answer now. It is a difficult thing for man to understand. In the explanation you will learn much about the Father, Heaven, and eternity. You have heard me say that man was not created for the Sabbath but that the Sabbath was created for man. Do you remember?"

"Yes, I remember that."

"Why do you think that is the case?"

"I suppose that because after six days of hard labor we need a rest."

"You have spoken wisely probably more wisely than you know."

"Yes, but what does that have to do with Judas?"

"You are right in saying that Judas will betray me. I know it. I know when and how he will do it."

"But that is not possible. He has not yet done it."

"Oh, but he will. When you answered that the Sabbath was created for man's rest after six days of labor you said something profound. You introduced the concept of time into our discussion."

Lazarus continued to climb contemplating what Jesus said. "But how can time be profound? We are all the captive of our time."

"As mortal men we are but the Father is not. When the Father told Moses His name is I Am, he told him that time did not matter. Time like the Sabbath was created for man. It means nothing to the Father. All time is the same. So when I tell you that I know Judas will betray me it is because he already has. The Father knows everything. Some might say he knows things that have not yet happened but that would be an error. He knows because everything that has been or will ever be happens simultaneously."

"I don't understand." Lazarus had stopped and now turned to look into the face of his friend.

"I know. I told you that it would not be easy. For the Father, you and I were born and died in the same moment. That is the same moment as when all of creation came into being—the stars, the earth, even Satan. When Satan revolted and led a third of the angels with him that was the same moment. So too was the fall of Adam and Eve when all the earth became corrupted. When I was in heaven with the Father, I saw everything that each man would do throughout his life. Now that I have come to earth as a man, I have lived as a man, subject to the same temptations and trials as any other man. To do otherwise would render my coming futile. That too is a great mystery, but let us now just talk of time and how the Father knows all things."

"But how do you know what Judas will do? Surely he has a free will and can change his mind. Or is he—we—all of us just so many puppets on a string, doing what we must?"

Jesus smiled. Lazarus had a spiritual gift for asking the right question at the right time. "No, man is not a puppet. Each man does exercise free will. Because all time is the same to the Father, He sees the end and knows the decisions that each of us will make even though we are free to decide for ourselves."

"I believe I see," Lazarus said, "but that still doesn't tell me how you know what Judas will do. You said when you came to earth that you live as a man. How can you know all this?"

"I know because the Father has told me. As a man, the Holy Spirit guided me in the early days of my earthly mission. Now I know because the Father and I are one just as the Spirit is with us — a Holy Trinity."

"When, when did you know?"

"The Holy Spirit has always been with me, but as a man I became aware of His presence when I was just twelve years of age. We went to the temple for Passover as I told you. Something happened to me then that as a boy I did not fully understand. What I did understand were the Scriptures so I engaged in conversation with the learned men who served there. At the river when I went to be baptized by John the Spirit revealed more. Even as you have been with me things have been revealed. For that reason I am sometimes not understood. Now I see it all and for that reason I want to spend these few days with you and your sisters. I want to enjoy this human life before I do what must be done."

Lazarus began climbing the road once more. They were now nearing the top of the climb, and night had fallen. The cliff still obscured the sky but the full moon and the stars illuminated their path. Lazarus was reminded of another psalm that said that God's word would be a lamp to his feet and a light to his path. Walking and talking to Jesus allowed him to see.

"So then, the Father talks to you?"

"Oh yes. When I talk to Him, as you have seen me pray, He answers. As a small boy the Father entrusted me to Joseph and my mother. They guided me in what I was to do and say. They taught me the Scriptures. When I became a man His Spirit began guiding me. It was the Holy Spirit that led me to the river the day we first met. Even then I knew that you would have a significant role to play in my mission on earth although until recently I did not know what that would be."

"So then you know what will happen to me and my sisters?"

"Of course I know that you worry but you have no reason to. You and they will be with me in eternity."

"But what does that mean, eternity?"

"Men who are constrained by their concepts of time like to think of it as all the time there is when there simply isn't any more time, but that is an error. Eternity has nothing to do with time. It is a state of being."

Again, Lazarus was confused. "I don't understand. I know that I am just a simple man, but that is so hard."

Jesus wanted his friend to understand, so he said, "The things of the Father are beyond mere man's ability to fathom.

As men we are limited by words. The Father and I do not have that limitation but in dealing with men we use words as well as visions. Some men say that heaven will be a place where we will sing praises to the Father all the time. I tell you that the reality of how men will spend eternity goes far beyond that. It is being in a continual state of bliss. Consider the happiest, the most satisfying, the most pleasurable, and the most content moment in your life. Then consider that all the ecstasy you have experienced during your lifetime was captured in a single moment and never left you. If you can imagine that then you will have some idea of what Heaven is like. Eternity in Heaven will be all that and more. It will not be limited by time. It will be an existence in the presence of the Father!"

"But what about those you said will be consigned to Hell?"

"Hell is an awful place. There, the lost souls will be aware of the same things that those in Heaven are enjoying only they will be denied them. They will know that the joy they have lost is being in the presence of the Father. Nothing can be worse than that. So when I talk about Hell being a place of fire and burning flesh it is because that is the worst pain man can imagine. But I want you to understand that Hell is much worse. To know the Father, to come before Him for the judgment, and then to be denied His presence is the worst thing that can happen to a soul. And it will never end.

It will never end because time does not exist. Those souls will simply be in a state of being where they will experience the worst kind of agony. Those people will exist without joy or peace because they rejected me."

They had reached the top of the cliff. The clear night sky was ablaze with God's creation. The light God that had set for them at night illuminated the earth making their path easy to follow. Lazarus observed it and knew the horribly wrong path Judas followed. "Is there any hope for Judas?"

"Yes. He has free will. He can follow a different path if he wants. You and your sisters will be with me and the Father in eternity. That will be enough for you because there is no greater reward that that. Just as the time we will now spend together is greater than the errand I have sent the others to perform this time is to prepare you and your sisters for the glory that will come next."

They said nothing more but continued walking toward the house on the hill outside Bethany. A little more than an hour later they reached the house. The door had been closed and barred against the cold night air. Lazarus stopped at the clay water jug outside the house on the wooden bench while Jesus walked to the door and knocked.

A woman's voice, wary because of the late hour, called out from the other side. "Who is there?"

"A weary traveler and his friend, we are in search of a place to stay for the night," Jesus answered playfully. Then, motioning to Lazarus, he said, "You had better speak up. They are uneasy at someone coming to the house so late."

"Mary, Martha, it is I, Lazarus. I have brought Jesus with me."

The sound of the bar being removed from the door resonated a moment before the women rushed out and threw arms around their brother. A moment later they turned to look at the man who they knew had come to save all Israel.

"We are honored to welcome you to our home." Martha said.

Taking the water jug from Lazarus they washed the dust off the men's feet. They had heard about the miracles performed by Jesus but were astonished at how ordinary he seemed. They talked well into the night, the women wanting to know how their brother had fared during his long absence. Sometime after midnight Mary looked over and noticed that Jesus had fallen asleep. Not wishing to disturb him they extinguished the lamp and lifted his feet onto the couch leaving him to sleep there until morning. The man they knew as a friend far from both his earthly and heavenly homes had chosen to celebrate Hanukkah with them out of all the people in Israel.

Whispering so that they would not awaken their guest they anxiously discussed what they had in the house that would make a suitable gift for him. At last they took a piece of parchment and wrote these words: "We know you are the long-awaited Messiah and we give our lives to you." All three siblings then signed the parchment and lit the celebration lamp using the most precious oil of all. After that, they spent a restless night waiting for Jesus to find their gift.

Chapter 17

Peter and Andrew came to Bethany at the end of the eight-day celebration. Not finding Jesus at the home of Lazarus they searched for him at the Temple where he had gone several times during in the week without being noticed. Here far away from Galilee without the crowds surrounding him, where he did not perform any miracles, he blended into the mass of people visiting the Temple Mount every day. On those visits he and Lazarus walked freely around the inner courts. Jesus stopped at the entrance to the Holy of Holies and smelled the aroma of the smoke from the sacrifices. He looked at the doorway and saw the curtain representing the separation of this world from God. Lazarus noticed a wistful expression on his face.

Leaving the Holy of Holies they saw Peter and Andrew. Now he shed the cloak of anonymity and spoke openly in Solomon's colonnade. He restored sight to a man who had been born blind. Not satisfied with this the crowd began to gather and question him asking, "How long will you keep us in suspense? If you are the Christ, tell us plainly."

Jesus answered, *"I have already told you, and you don't believe me. The proof is in the miracles I do in the name of my Father. But you don't believe me because you are not part of my flock. My sheep recognize my voice, I know them and they follow me. I give them eternal life and they shall never perish. No one shall snatch them away from me because my Father has given them to me and no one can kidnap them from me. I and the Father are one."* Once more Jesus had answered them but they were not satisfied. He left.

Returning to Bethany he announced that he along with Peter and Andrew would be leaving the following day. When Lazarus questioned him why he would not be permitted to go with them, Jesus answered, "It is because of your health that you should not return. Your service to me will be here in Bethany. Before the Passover you will be a miracle showing the world the way."

Lazarus did not understand. "The way where Lord?"

"Why, the way to me of course," was all that Jesus would answer. "Your faith is well known here. Your life and mine are now woven together in the minds of the people in Jerusalem and the surrounding towns. They have seen us together and know us to be friends."

Lazarus asked for more. "But when will you come back?"

"You will leave before I return. First you will not know where you have gone and then you will." Speaking now in the mysterious manner he used so often, he continued. "You will hear my voice calling to you and you will not want to come. But come you will to the glory of God."

Lazarus thought back to the dream he had when he and Judas spent the night in Jericho three years earlier. Could that be what Jesus meant?

"I will do whatever you say." He had no idea how profound his answer would prove to be.

Jesus, Peter, and Andrew departed the following morning to meet with the others at the predetermined place for them to reassemble.

Time passed slowly for Lazarus after they left. His health which had been so robust while in the presence of Jesus began to deteriorate. The headaches and weakness returned. Reports of Jesus' teaching and miracles flowed in to Bethany on a daily basis. He taught about prayer—not just what it was but how to do it, what to say. He attacked the Pharisees and the religious leaders for their hypocrisy.

Six times he cried out: "Woe to you Pharisees, and you other religious leaders. Hypocrites!"

As the reports continued Lazarus could not help but wonder if Jesus was now intentionally trying to provoke them. He wondered why Jesus singled out the Pharisees to the exclusion of the Sadducees. The Sadducees did not even believe in the resurrection. The Pharisees at least believed in that and taught many of the same things that Jesus did even though the inspiration for their instruction was different. Their teaching came from man while Jesus' came from the Spirit. Lazarus understood that Jesus did not intend his words against the Pharisees to apply to every member of that sect. After all he had many friends and followers who identified themselves with the Pharisees. Nicodemus and Joseph of Arimathea were members of the Sanhedrin and they were Pharisees. Jesus called those men his friends. Jesus accused the Pharisees as a group for another reason.

Lazarus wondered it if had something to do with time or the absence of it that Jesus knew. Then, one day a stranger came to Bethany and repeated what he had heard Jesus say to his disciples about trusting God and the judgment that awaited all mankind. *"I have come to bring fire to the earth, and, oh, that my task were completed! There is a terrible baptism ahead of me, and how I am pent up until it is accomplished! Do you think I have come to give peace to the earth? No! Rather, strife and division! From now on families will be split apart, three in favor of me, and two against—or perhaps the other way around. A father will decide one way about me; his son, the other; mother and daughter will disagree; and the decision of an honored mother-in-law will be spurned by her daughter-in-law." "Brother shall betray brother to death, and fathers shall betray their own children. And children shall rise against their parents and cause their deaths. Everyone shall hate you because you belong to me. But all of you who endure to the end shall be saved."* The disciples had argued about what he meant. Surely the nation was united against the Romans. Why would he talk about the division of father against son and mother against daughter? And Jews killing Jews; what did that have to do with Rome?

Did he or did he not intend to lead a revolt against the Romans?

Winter had now given way to the promise of spring. Jesus used the occasion to chide the people for their lack of understanding about who had sent him and what that meant. He pointed out that as the signs of the changing season appeared they understood what was about to happen. He concluded by telling them, *"You are good at reading the weather signs of the skies—red sky tonight means fair weather tomorrow; red sky in the morning means foul weather all day—but you can't read the obvious signs of the times! This evil, unbelieving nation is asking for some strange sign in the heavens, but no further proof will be given except the miracle that happened to Jonah."* Judas becoming more arrogant in his own interpretation of these teachings, incorporated them in the document he now titled The Gospel of Judas.

He drew attention to just how corrupt they were. He reflected that they were like the whitewashed tombs that covered the eastern side of the Kiddron Valley within sight of the temple, saying, *"Woe to you, teachers of the law and Pharisees, you hypocrites! You are like whitewashed tombs. They look beautiful on the outside but on the inside are full of dead men's bones and everything unclean. In the same way, on the outside you appear to people as righteous but on the inside you are full of hypocrisy and wickedness."*

Lazarus knew that these words were inflaming the religious leaders against Jesus and heard rumors that they now plotted to kill him. He wanted to find his friend and tell him what he heard but could not. His health had worsened dramatically in the waning days of winter. Hardly a week passed when he did not have an attack of headache, confusion or instability. While these episodes did not last more than a day or two they increased in number. The interval between them decreased.

A week later, when his sisters awakened him, he could not see. He soon fell asleep again. He slept without waking for a full day. When he did awaken again he could not talk. Later in the day he lapsed into what they knew was not sleep but a coma.

No longer able to get any response from him they sent a message to Jesus who had returned to the area saying, "Sir, your good friend is very, very sick." Hours after sending word by messenger they entered the room where their brother lay. He was dead.

Jesus received the message without comment and continued what he had been doing. Two days later the disciples who had grown fond of Lazarus urged Jesus to go and see what had happened to their friend. Jesus answered them, saying, *"The purpose of his illness is not death, but for the glory of God...Our friend Lazarus has gone to sleep, but now I will go and waken him!"*

Relieved to hear this they changed their minds saying, "That means he is getting better!"

Jesus wanted them to understand what he meant, and he spoke to them so that they would understand. *"Lazarus is dead. And for your sake, I am glad I wasn't there, for this will give you another opportunity to believe in me. Come, let's go to him."*

The disciples appeared puzzled by this comment, yet they were overjoyed to know that their Master intended to do something. Only Judas, recalling how Jesus had raised the boy at Nain and suspected Jairus' daughter had not been dead but asleep as Jesus had said at the time, harbored bad feelings about this journey. Lazarus had once been his friend but jealousy now filled his heart. Jesus paid more attention to him.

Chapter 18

The large stone at the entrance to the tomb kept out all light. Even so, the light he saw was brighter than anything he had ever seen. He had never known such peace and joy. The source of the light seemed to come from somewhere before him illuminating a world much like the one he had left though somehow different. He knew his spirit had escaped the grave and he had come to a perfect world. He recognized the place as Bethany but it had been transformed. Perfection, the kind of perfection that only God could know surrounded him. The source of the light generated a fullness of love he had never before experienced. Strangest of all he knew that Jesus waited for him in the light. He could not fathom how that could be. He had died but Jesus lived. How could Jesus be in both places at the same time? Then he recalled what Jesus had said about time. Time was created for man. God was eternal. Could that explain it?

A soothing voice said. "You are home. You will spend eternity here with us." Inside the tomb the dead man did not so much hear the voice but became aware of the manifestation of eternity calling to him. Then the voice spoke again. It was the voice of God. It was the voice of his friend Jesus speaking in a commanding tone, *"Lazarus, come forth!"*

He hesitated. Jesus had just told him he would spend

eternity with God and now he commanded him to come out of the grave. In the instant of his hesitation he knew what he would do. He swung both feet off the cold limestone slab where his dead body lay and stood. Then walking out into the sunlight, dim and pale by comparison to the warm brilliance he had just left, he stood while two of his friends began removing the cloth that bound him in death. He had been dead but now he lived again.

The recollection of the dream at Jericho now made sense. This was the dream. This is what he dreamed long ago. He did not want to leave, and yet he did. He had been home, truly at home, and had not wanted to return to this world of gloom, despair, and betrayal, a world of pain and suffering where your friend one day would become your enemy the next. Yet, when Jesus called to him he came. He had told his friend that he would do whatever he commanded and he had done it. He had left the comfort of heaven to return to this fallen world where sin corrupted what God had made perfect.

He looked around and saw Judas standing at the edge of the crowd with a gleam like fire in his eyes, a look that could kill. He wanted to tell him that he was wrong. He had been in heaven itself. Barbelo and Saklas did not exit. They were mere foolishness planted by God's ultimate enemy, an enemy destined to destruction. He wanted to tell Judas that if he persisted on that path he would suffer the same destiny but he could not. He remembered a voice, Jesus, telling him that

Judas must decide for himself. He had a free will and could choose whatever path he wanted.

Jesus spoke to him again. This time the voice came from his friend and not God. How that could be confused him. Jesus was God and Man at the same time. "Come. Let's return to your house so that Mary and Martha can prepare breakfast for us. My companions and I have been on the road since early this morning and have had nothing to eat. And you my friend must be hungry after your ordeal."

But he was not hungry. He had not eaten for a week before he died and had been in the grave for four days and yet he did not want food.

Jesus continued in a quiet voice only he could hear. "It will be all right. You should eat. I know that you don't want or need food now but it is for their sake that I am telling them to prepare food. We will eat; I because I am hungry, you because they need to know that although you were dead you are truly alive. They need to know that you are not an aberration. Only a living person can eat."

Judas lagged behind as the others walked away. He felt excluded by the other eleven disciples. He knew they suspected him of stealing from their treasury. He resented their condemnation even though he did in fact help himself to whatever it contained. And why shouldn't he? They were fools for following Saklas the god of fools while he and Jesus were the only true believers. He had staked everything the past year on that belief and now he did not know what to think. If Jesus wanted to die in order to show the others the way to Barbelo why did he raise Lazarus? And what was the laughter all about as they walked through the village? Were they laughing at him? Had he been played for a fool all along? The thought that Jesus and the others had been playing a monstrous joke on him caused his blood to boil. He hesitated alongside the road. It was then that the man whom he had noticed following them approached.

"Judas," the man said as he reached out, placing his hand on the shoulder of the disenchanted disciple, "what is it that just happened back there?"

"Who are you?" He looked at the man thinking I've seen him before, but where? At Gerasa, that is where. He was there when Jesus ridiculed him in front of everyone. He stared at the man wearing everyday clothing but otherwise had the appearance of someone in authority. If for no other reason the incongruity in the man's dress and appearance raised his suspicions.

"My name isn't important, but the people who sent me are." He stopped short of saying he had been sent by the high priest.

"So?"

"I have noticed that the others do not respect you. They leave you out of their discussions whenever they can. I may have been observing from afar, but whenever I am close in the crowd you are always the farthest away from Jesus."

"That's true. They don't like me because I am not like them. I came from Judah. They are all from Galilee. I am certain that they would cut me off from all contact with Jesus if they could."

"That is what I have observed." He skillfully moved from observation to manipulation. "I don't see where they have much to brag about, being from Galilee." He smiled an ingratiating smile. "You were so much closer to what just happened than I. What did just happen?"

"Jesus just raised that man. He was dead, and now he is alive."

Something showed on the man's face. What was it: shock, surprise, confirmation? "Are you certain?"

"Of course I am certain. The man he raised is named Lazarus. He was a friend of mine. Jesus knew that he would die days before he actually did. Even then he did nothing. He wanted to let Lazarus lie in that tomb until his body began to decay before coming here."

"You say that he raised him from being dead. How can that be?"

"Don't ask me. He just stood outside the tomb after we rolled away the stone and he told him to come out. That is what I saw. When he did come out there was that awful stench of death. When two of the disciples removed his burial clothes he had the body of a healthy and vigorous man."

"That is impossible," the man replied.

"That may be but that is what happened. Jesus said he is the Son of God. I suppose that could explain it. Weren't the prophets of olden times reported to do many miraculous things?" Judas in his confusion did not elaborate on his version of the ancient writings.

The man inched closer. The jubilant crowd surrounding Jesus and Lazarus were now nearly out of sight. The sounds of happiness no longer reverberated in the still air. "And what do you think of all this?"

Judas realized that the words were not so much a question as an indictment. "They are all fools."

The man replied. "I must go into the city and make my report. Watch for me during the Passover week. I will be close by if you ever want to talk." The man squeezed his hand on Judas's shoulder as a sign of friendship and departed taking the road to Jerusalem.

That road led to the edge of a steep precipice, the rim of the Kiddron Valley. A vast olive grove spread out behind him. The man stopped. The sight of the city and its walls on the other side thrilled him. From where he now stood he could see across the valley to the Temple Mount. His eyes drifted across the walls of the ancient city. Just to the right and halfway up the valley on the other side he could see the Eastern Gate, the main entrance into the city from this road.

To his left he saw the Temple shrouded in smoke from the daily sacrifices being offered to God. He looked further north and saw his destination, the palace of the high priest.

He stepped over the edge began the steep descent. Then his momentum caused him to run down the road toward the valley floor. He passed a place of dread. The sight of it always gave him an eerie feeling. The road followed the border of a massive cemetery that stretched as far as his eye could see if he had been inclined to look in that direction. The tombs of the Jews all the way back to the prophets including those who had been murdered at Jerusalem were here. Some were marked by ornate edifices and others mere slabs of whitewashed granite or limestone.

The cemetery had been the place that Jesus had gestured to when he attacked the Pharisees, telling them that they were like whitewashed tombs all clean on the outside but full of dead bones and corruption on the inside.

He stumbled and fell as he raced down the steep hill. Even in the light of day the place frightened him. He brushed himself off and hurried forward struggling to stay under control on the descent to the Eastern Gate. Entering the city, he followed the winding streets until at last he found the stairs he recognized. The worn steps led up to the palace located near the juncture of the Kiddron Valley and the Valley of Hinnom, also known as Gehenna, the place of refuse where fires burned day and night blending the aroma of the temple with the stench of burning garbage.

At the top he followed the path around to the front door of the palace. A guard stopped him. "I've come to see Caiaphas," he asserted.

"He isn't here," the guard replied. "You will have to talk to his counsel. He's here."

The door opened.

The man entered. A Jew from Tarsus who studied the law under Gamaliel, the Sanhedrin presiding officer, received him. The lawyer greeted the man with cool detachment. A spy was not the sort of man he chose for an associate. Nevertheless, even spies had their place and the information they brought often proved to be valuable to the high priest.

"It is about time you returned. You have been gone for weeks and we have not had any word from you. Have you learned anything or have you wasted the temple money?"

The man bristled at the indictment. Caiaphas never treated him in that manner. "I have learned much," he answered biting back his bitterness at the treatment.

"Well, what is it. We pay for information and that is what we expect. What have you learned?" he repeated.

Looking at the stern expression chiseled on the face of his misshapen interrogator he replied, "The man Jesus is even more dangerous to the high priest than anyone imagined. He has powers that could only come from Satan himself." Or God, he thought. The power could come from God but that is not what they want to hear. "This very morning he raised the olive merchant from Bethany."

"What do you mean he raised him? Where was he?"

"Dead; the man was dead!"

The lawyer stood in disbelief digesting the information. "Are you certain?"

"Of course I am certain. I was there. I talked with one of his disciples, a man by the name of Judas. Judas stood at the entrance of the tomb when the man came out. I had to stand some distance off and could not see or hear everything for myself. My orders were to be discreet." The man continued. "I had to stand well away from the cemetery but I did see the man come out of the tomb wrapped in a shroud. From the reaction of the men with Jesus they wanted nothing to do with the body, dead or not. They did eventually remove the burial wrapping from the man and he walked away with Jesus."

"How did you come to have this conversation with the man Judas?"

"Judas has become disillusioned with Jesus and he is jealous of the others. Judas and the..." he struggled to find the right word..."dead man Lazarus were friends at one time. But when Jesus began replacing Judas with Lazarus the friendship dissolved. At least in the mind of Judas it has."

"And?"

"Judas did not immediately follow the others. I could tell

that something about the event bothered him. I approached him and he talked freely. I believe that he could be of use to us in the future."

The lawyer did not like the use of the word us in the context of a spy acting in concert with the high priest Caiaphas and his counsel. Reluctantly, the counsel spoke words of praise. "You have done well. I will report what you have learned to the high priest and the Sanhedrin." With those words he dismissed the spy and immediately went to work organizing a meeting of the members of the Sanhedrin.

The meeting took place across the city from the palace of the high priest near the temple. Friends or supporters of Jesus and any member of the ruling council not openly sharing the view of the high priest concerning Jesus were excluded.

The meeting commenced with the legal counsel to the high priest, Saul of Tarsus, making an opening statement. He bowed to the high priest and the presiding officer of the Sanhedrin seated on a raised dais in matching thrones. "We have gathered today in extraordinary session to take up a matter of utmost importance to the security of our institutions and the people."

The members murmured among themselves not having been told the purpose of the meeting in advance. They had not been invited. They had been summoned by the two most powerful Jewish men in the land.

Raising his hand to reestablish order he continued. "We are here to consider recent events surrounding the man Jesus from Nazareth. First, let me summarize what we know about the man's past activities." He paused for dramatic effect. "Almost from the first moment he came to our attention he has caused trouble. Three years ago he came to the temple at Passover and created a disturbance by assaulting merchants conducting their lawful business on the Temple Mount. Had he not left the area we would have taken action against him at that time. On his departure he joined with the religious fanatic John baptizing people in the Jordan River. A dispute arose between the two rival factions. Trouble there was only averted when John agreed to take a subservient role. Eventually this man Jesus returned to Galilee where he reportedly performed several so-called miracles of healing and other tricks like turning water into wine."

Laughter broke out among the members. One of them cried out, "That sounds like a man I could like."

The others laughed even harder.

Gamaliel pounded his scepter on the floor to restore order, the scowl of reproof serving as ample warning against additional outbursts.

The lawyer continued. "He traveled over a wide area, preaching. In time, he claimed to be the Messiah often referring to himself as the Son of Man and even the Son of God. At his home in Nazareth he claimed to be the fulfillment of the prophecy made by Isaiah. As a result of that the people in his home synagogue tried to kill him. Since that time, there have been claims that he has cured people suffering from incurable diseases. It has been claimed that he raised people from the dead. We have not been able to substantiate any of these claims.

"Recently he has begun attacking the institutions of our faith. You members of the Pharisees who constitute the Sanhedrin have been the object of some of his most vicious attacks. If he succeeds in these attacks the very institution of the Sanhedrin and even that of the high priest will be threatened. And make no mistake. These attacks have been successful. Great numbers of the population are going over to him."

The lawyer paused for the fact to sink in. Then, pulling his twisted body to his full height, his voice rose in crescendo. "And now, word from a reliable source has reached us that he has truly done the impossible. We have a report from one of our own agents that, even as close as Bethany, he has done something only Satan himself can do. He has raised a man, dead for four days, from the cold dark tomb a man whose flesh had begun to rot. The man he restored to life is someone known to us, a man by the name of Lazarus. Some of you may even know him. If we let him go on like this everyone will believe in him. Then the Romans will come and take away both our place and our nation. I ask you, what should we make of this event? How should we respond to it?"

He sat, smirking, exulting in the manner with which he had manipulated the facts to arouse the suspicion and anger of his listeners. He looked up at the high priest and presiding officer. They both nodded their approval as the chamber erupted.

"Do away with the high priest, never!"

"He would destroy the Sanhedrin!"

"The people are like sheep to be led astray by false teaching. We must do something to silence this man."

"Who should rule the people if not us?"

The presiding officer allowed the disorganized shouting to continue for as long as the assembled members vented their opinions. When at last their shouting subsided, he spoke.

"We need to hear from the high priest. Caiaphas, what do you say?"

So far, the script that Caiaphas, Gamaliel, and the lawyer had laid out that afternoon had been perfectly executed.

The high priest Caiaphas rose from his throne and stepped forward two paces before stopping. He stood casting his glance over each of the twenty faces assembled in the room before beginning. Wanting to be seen as contemplative and deliberate in judgment he raised his hands as if in supplication to God. "We are all troubled by these reports. There have been so many rumors that we have not been able to verify concerning this man. Now this! What are we to make of it? Up until today his assaults have been on us as individuals. Of course we are offended. Who would not be? But this! If the reports are true then he must be in concert with the devil himself. It would not be the first time the people have been led astray and followed false teaching to their destruction. The One whose name I cannot mention will not permit such heresy. As the moral guides to the people it is our sacred obligation to see that does not happen. Because the people have been misled in earlier times our predecessors instituted rules governing these matters. But what can we do? Aren't our hands tied by the Romans? In the olden times we would have brought this man before us and tried him for his crimes and if, I repeat if, he was found guilty he would be taken out and stoned. Alas, that is no longer an option for us. Rome will not permit it."

He dropped his head forward, the miter on his head nearly falling off as his chin rested on his chest. Dropping his hands to his sides he backed to his throne and sat.

Instantly, the clamor began anew. Shouts of "Kill him!" were heard. "Forget the Romans and a trial. Kill him. Do away with him. We don't need to have a trial. Send the temple guards to kill him."

Gamaliel rose to speak. "No. We cannot involve the guards in this matter. There must be another way."

A man at the back of the room shouted out, "What can

we do? Our hands are tied."

Caiaphas, with a look of resignation again lifted his hand to quiet them. "You stupid idiots—let this one man die for the people—why should the whole nation perish?"

From the back of the room, someone shouted out, "What about Lazarus?"

Caiaphas answered, "He too must die. If he is allowed to live the people will believe everything that Jesus said. Once Jesus is dead, Lazarus too must die!"

The voice from the back questioned, "But how, when?"

Caiaphas looked out over the faces of his co-conspirators. "We will consider that. We have a willing partner in one of his disciples. We will watch and wait for our opportunity. In the meantime, both Jesus and Lazarus will be closely watched."

Chapter 19

Jesus knew the temple leaders and Sanhedrin would consider him a threat to their continued rule. Because of that and the fact that it was not time for him to complete his earthly mission, he and the twelve disciples left Bethany. He led them north along the mountain ridge through Samaria where earlier he had talked to a woman at a village well. He selected this route knowing the path would deter anyone from the Temple who might be following him.

Lazarus once more found himself excluded after being told to remain in Bethany and go about his business in an ordinary manner. Lazarus, not knowing what to expect, asked Eliazar to continue serving the family as steward out of loyalty for the service he had already provided. Eliazar appeared to be surprised. The man had his life and health restored. Lazarus had never appeared to be so vigorous. He seemed to have a perfect body. He did not tire. He did not become thirsty or hungry although he did eat and drink from time to time. Lazarus recognized his altered state. He stood awed by the power of Jesus who had explained so much on the long walk up the Jericho road and on the way back from the tomb to the house. But, for Lazarus, there were more questions than answers in that discourse. The world he now walked appeared even more evil than the one he left when he died. Why had he been commanded to leave the splendor of that other world? He wondered what would happen to mankind. God had a plan for mankind's destiny, but more than that He cared for each individual. He understood it was Jesus, not the Law given by Moses or the regulations of the Pharisees that gave him that certainty.

Time passed. The month of Adar gave way to Nisan, the first month of the Jewish calendar dating from the peoples' deliverance from bondage in Egypt. The mood of people soared with anticipation. Excitement in the village had as much to do with the unusually good weather as the coming Passover fifteen days distant. No word concerning Jesus had been received for over two weeks. It almost seemed that he had vanished but the family knew he would return for Passover. It had been his lifelong custom and so they watched every day for his return. He had gone on the high road toward Samaria but they watched both that road and the Jericho road. They had no way of knowing that even as they waited and watched he had already begun his journey toward Jerusalem.

Suddenly, he was there. He smiled as he approached with the disciples following behind. "Shalom aleichem, my friends."

The greeting warmed Lazarus. "Aleichem Shalom. I know that it has only been a few weeks since you left but I have missed you. We watched for your return but thought something had happened. There are rumors. The Pharisees in the Sanhedrin are plotting to kill you. It is said that they want to kill me as well."

"Do not be concerned about such things. The Father has a plan. It will all work itself out according to His will."

"Then you intend to go to the city for the Passover?"

"Of course, but first I will stay the night with you."

Hearing those words, Mary and Martha hurried to the house and began preparing a dinner in Jesus' honor. Soon, word of Jesus' arrival spread and a crowd gathered outside the house. Martha served. When the dinner ended Mary took a jar of pure nard, an expensive perfume, poured it on Jesus' feet and wiped his feet with her hair. The house filled with the fragrance.

Judas objected. "That perfume was worth a fortune. It should have been sold and the money given to the poor."

Jesus replied. "Let her alone. She did it in preparation for my burial. You can always help the poor, but I won't be with you much longer."

A large crowd had gathered outside the house hoping to see both Jesus and Lazarus. One man known only to Judas and Jesus stood off to the side, the spy who had approached Judas weeks earlier.

The following morning, Jesus sent two of his disciples into Bethany on an errand. They returned some time later with a young donkey for their master to ride into the city.

Before leaving Jesus drew Lazarus close. "You may accompany me down to Jerusalem but do not enter the city. Go home and wait. My Father will summon you when it is time."

"But how will I know?" Lazarus objected. "The Father has never spoken to me."

"His Spirit will tell you when it is time to come. When he does, come without waiting. Don't worry. You will be with friends you have not seen for a long time."

The throng of people surrounding the house watched as Jesus mounted the colt then, with Lazarus and his sisters in the vanguard, led the way to the road leading to Jerusalem. Soon the voices of a thousand people singing God's praise could be heard over the hills. At the precipice where the spy had lingered, Jesus stopped. He wept then went down the steep road beside the vast cemetery toward the Eastern Gate.

Lazarus stopped and watched as Jesus passed by not knowing if or when he would see him again.

Five days later, hours before the Sabbath and Passover began, Lazarus heard a voice. He noted for the first time the coincidence of Passover falling on the Sabbath and wondered about the significance. The voice told him to go into Jerusalem by the Sheep Gate and proceed through the city. A half hour before three o'clock in the afternoon he left home without saying anything to his sisters and walked the same path he had taken when they led the procession.

The day had started clear and bright but dark clouds now gathered over the city of David. At the edge of the precipice he too stopped. He looked at the Temple Mount covered with a dark foreboding cloud. Somewhere off to the west he saw another cloud. The two clouds seemed to be converging. Something was happening in the city.

He walked down the steep road a place of triumph five days earlier. As he did so, the stone covers of countless whitewashed tombs began to move. Men and women who had been dead for years rose up to join him. He recognized the wife of a neighbor who had died six years earlier. No longer dead she had the appearance of a woman in midlife, healthy and alive. Other old friends joined him moments later. All had been faithful to God and had not fallen away under the evil influence of their corrupt leaders. Tears of joy filled his eyes at the bottom of the hill when he caught up with his wife and child, his mother and father—all vigorous and in the prime of life. They walked past the Eastern Gate that led directly to the Temple Mount as if they realized that the temple no longer represented the dwelling place of God. They went north along the valley floor to the Sheep Gate. This entrance led to the Fortress Antonio and from there down a broad street that wound its way through the ancient city until it came out at the Town Gate.

They followed the street that one day would bear the

name Via Doloroso, the Way of Sorrow. No one seemed to notice anything different about them. They were simply a group of people, more healthy in appearance than most, who had come to the crowded city for Passover. They exited the city through the broad arched gate leading to Damascus. Across the road they saw the garden belonging to Joseph of Arimethea and above it the dreaded hill known as the place of the skull, Golgotha. From the road Lazarus and the others saw the human remnant of the divine body hanging on the cross. Lazarus gasped. "So much evil has killed so much love."

Having borne witness to the completion of God's plan, they reentered the city and proceeded back to their homes where they could tell their friends and families all they had seen and experienced.

Five days later two travelers returning to Jerusalem from Emmaus stopped at a house outside Bethany cloaked in unimaginable sadness and joy. A wall seemed to have been constructed in time. All of history was on one side with everything in the future on the other. Lazarus saw the men walking in his direction. "Peace upon you," he said. "What is the news? The entire world seems to be holding its breath."

"You could not be more right," the older man answered. "The streets of Jerusalem were vacant when we left the city early Sunday morning. Everyone seemed exhausted from the strange events that occurred before the Sabbath. There were even rumors of vandalism at the temple. It seems that the curtain in the Holy of Holies was torn ripped from top to bottom."

Tears welled in Lazarus's eyes. "And what is the news of Jesus of Nazareth and his disciples. They were my friends."

The wary expression on the younger man's face vanished. He answered. "Nothing of the disciples but we too are followers of Jesus. The most wonderful thing happened to us on our way to Emmaus from the city."

The older man dropped all reserve and spoke freely. "Wonderful is hardly the word for it. Forgive me for not telling you immediately but the open hostility toward Jesus and his followers made me pause."

"Yes, I understand. What is the news?"

The man clasped Lazarus by the shoulders and hugged him. "He is alive."

"Who is alive; Peter and John are alive? I thought they might be killed next."

"No. It is not them I mean. Jesus is alive. We have seen him. A man walked with us all the way to Emmaus. He wanted to know why we were sad, so we told him, 'The things that happened to Jesus, the man from Nazareth. He was a prophet who did incredible miracles and was a mighty teacher, highly regarded by both God and man. But the chief priests and our religious leaders arrested him and handed him over to the Roman government to be condemned to death, and they crucified him. We had thought that he was the glorious Messiah and that he had come to rescue Israel.' The man walking with us listened to what we said but when he answered, he said we were foolish for not understanding the teaching of the prophets. I swear to you that we did not know the man but we knew he had to be a teacher. His knowledge of Scripture exceeded that of any man we knew. When we got to the end of our journey we asked him to eat with us. We sat down and he blessed the bread. When he did we recognized him. The man was Jesus."

Lazarus felt a thrill run down his back from his head to his toes making the hair on his neck stand and chill bumps appear on his legs. "Where is he now?" he asked.

"We don't know. He disappeared. He appeared suddenly and vanished the same way. After he blessed the bread and we recognized him, he was gone."

"What are you going to do?" Lazarus wanted to know.

"I...we don't know. We are afraid of the Romans but even more afraid of our own leaders. They were entrusted by God to teach us the Law of Moses and to preside over our sacrifices. And yet they demanded that the Messiah be crucified. That is why we circled around the city so that we can enter from the east. Who knows, someone may have seen or heard something of what we have related. I would not have spoken to you about this if you had not first told us that you were his friend."

The man stopped and looked at Lazarus. "Who are you?" He had suddenly become aware of where it was he stood, on a hill outside Bethany just on the other side of the Mount of Olives.

"My name is Lazarus."

The men stumbled back. Not only had they seen the resurrected Jesus. Now, in the space of two days they stood before the man Jesus had raised from the dead weeks earlier. Mumbling words of departure they left heading toward the city now more confused than ever about what it was they should do.

Lazarus reentered his house and told the news to his sisters, his wife and child along with his mother and father.

The following day three disciples left Jerusalem hurrying toward Galilee. Andrew, his brother Simon Peter and the one Jesus playfully called Barley were following Jesus' instruction. I will meet you in Galilee he had said. When the disciples approached Bethany Lazarus recognized them and ran to meet them. "Peter, Andrew, Bartholomew, I have wonderful news. Jesus is alive."

"We know," Andrew answered. "He appeared to us in the upper room of Mark's house, but how did you know?"

"Two men returning to Jerusalem from Emmaus stopped yesterday and told me that they had seen him." He then related all he had heard.

When Andrew heard what the men had said about the high priest and religious leaders, he answered, "Possibly that is why the Master told us to meet him in Galilee."

Chapter 20

Forty days had passed since Jesus rose from the grave. Lazarus had been warned two days earlier that the Sanhedrin ordered temple guards to search for him. He could not imagine how they had failed to find him. He had not hidden from them. But now that they had found him he did not fear them. He stood his ground. After all what could they do to him? He had already died, had been dead. He knew what waited on the other side of the mysterious veil that frightened so many people. He knew that the bright light of the Lord of hosts had been, would again be, his reward.

Everyone who had known him since childhood understood that he was different. Jesus had touched his life in a way unlike any other. Now the man Jesus and Lazarus shared a common experience. Both had died yet both were alive. Jesus had risen as a personal testimony to the power of God, his power as God. He had come to earth to overcome death. But Jesus had gone from the grave in the garden tomb up to Galilee. Lazarus longed to see him again, to talk to him, to ask him to explain what would come next. From somewhere deep inside he thought he heard Jesus saying, "And just as it is destined that men die only once, and after that comes judgment, so also Christ died only once as an offering for the sins of many people; and he will come again, but not to deal again with our sins. This time he will come bringing salvation to all those who are eagerly and patiently waiting for him."

He expected there to be a judgment but he had not been judged when he died. Or had he? He had heard Jesus say just before being called from the tomb, "You are home. You will spend eternity here with us."

The reverie broke when someone spoke. "Are you Lazarus, the olive merchant from Bethany?"

"I am he," he responded. He looked around and saw that he stood in his olive orchard. He had no recollection of having come there but saw he had brought equipment with him so that he could work.

"Then it is you we are seeking." Without warning the soldier raised his spear and hurled it at Lazarus's chest having aimed directly at his heart.

Lazarus closed his eyes waiting for the sudden shock of the heavy weapon to strike. He did not fear death but in that instant before the impact he did fear dying. He had experience pain when he died the first time when he had experienced delirium. How much worse would the pain of dying be from a brutal attack?

The soldier watched the spear fly swiftly yet seemingly in slow motion. He had done it. He would be richly rewarded for removing the last living proof of the meddlesome carpenter. The spear appeared to move faster now only a few feet from where the man stood.

He watched in disbelief as the spear continued in flight falling harmlessly to the ground. Where had the man gone? He had been there in plain view one instant and gone the next. He moved forward, trembling. How could it be? The carpenter was dead, gone, his body stolen in the night by his crazed followers. Yet somehow the power he exerted continued. Could this be another of his miracles? The soldier had rejected all the rumors of miracles swirling around Jerusalem.

He and his companions, shocked, turned away in fear. This had to be witchcraft or the work of the devil. No man could simply disappear like that. There would be no reward. No, instead of reward they could look forward to punishment possibly death. The Sanhedrin would not allow them to live and tell this tale. "Say nothing about this to anyone," the spear thrower said. "Remember what happened to the soldiers who were sent to guard that tomb in the garden. I for one do not intend to explain that a dead man back from the grave just disappeared before my eyes. If you know what is good for you, you won't either."

Dropping their weapons and armor, one by one, no one speaking a word, they turned and walked back into the city with the hope that they could disappear into the crowd, not as Lazarus had disappeared but simply get lost in the teeming multitude.

At the very moment the temple guard hurled the spear at Lazarus' heart a scant mile to the west on the other side of the Mount of Olives a group of eleven men and three women stood in awe. The man the guard had thought of as a meddlesome carpenter had just finished speaking.

"I have been given all authority in heaven and earth. Therefore go and make disciples in all the nations, baptizing them into the name of the Father and of the Son and of the Holy Spirit, and then teach these new disciples to obey all the commands I have given you; and be sure of this—that I am with you always, even to the end of the world."

As the final phrase passed his lips, he was gone. They would later say that he was taken up into the clouds but they were never certain exactly what had happened. Words could not adequately describe the manner in which he left. One moment he was in their physical presence and the next he was gone. Something had happened to his physical body and when they thought back they remembered what he had said. *"Then all mankind will see me, the Messiah, coming in the clouds with great power and glory. And I will send out the angels to gather together my chosen ones from all over the world—from the farthest bounds of earth and heaven."*

When he had told them this weeks before it had seemed to be an exaggeration but now they had seen him go in just that way. At last it began to make sense.

Suddenly, they were together somewhere high above the Earth. Jesus and his friend Lazarus were together with all the people who had come out of their graves at the moment Jesus died on the cross. They were all there, his wife and child whom he had left with his sisters, his mother and father, the widow's son from Nain and many others who Lazarus recognized.

Lazarus looked down on the city of Jerusalem. Everything had been transformed. The city now spread out before him larger than he could imagine with streets appearing to me made of pure gold. "I don't understand. I seem to always be saying to you, 'I don't understand.' Where is the Jerusalem I know?"

"It is still there. I told you time only exists for mankind. This is what the Father and I saw at the moment of creation. This is reality. The other, the fallen world, is what mankind sees but not the Father. For the Father it has always been perfect because we made it to be perfect. Only a thin veil separates the two, like the curtain that separated the Holy Place from the Holy of Holies at the Temple. This is the place we created for us to be with man not a tabernacle or Temple. Everyone who accepts and acknowledges me as their Savior is here."

"But what about you; why did you have to be born, suffer, and die?"

"Because man sinned and he could never make himself worthy in the eyes of the Father. Man may be sorry for what he does but he will continue to sin. The only way for man to be restored to his creator was for God himself to make the sacrifice. The sacrifices that men could make would never be enough. From the very beginning, we knew it would be this way." Jesus smiled. "You see, everything I told you is true. And now we will be together beyond the grasp of time where bodies and minds can never grow old, become sick, or die. I knew we would be together when I saw you by the river so long ago. You were different from the moment I called you forth from the grave. You had a resurrected body. You still have one. You will be with me in the new Jerusalem where you will live in glory, you and all who accept my gift in time to come." He chuckled at the use of the word time. He looked to see if Lazarus understood. God had a sense of humor.

They began to descend from the clouds back toward earth but the closer they came the more it changed. The city of Jerusalem now spread out in all directions farther than the eye could see a vast gleaming beautiful city filled with light and promise. Only Jesus could now see the world they had left behind. His work on earth had been accomplished but His interest remained for those in that other dimension, the one created for man alone and measured in time. His Spirit would direct the work of those He left to see that all was accomplished.

Lazarus looked around. He saw more people joining them and it occurred to him that he knew each one by name. He had not known any of those people when he had walked the earth, the other earth, the one they had left. Even more surprising was the fact that he not only knew them but he knew that they were all there. Then sadness overwhelmed him but only for an instant. "Where is Judas? I do not see Judas."

Jesus answered, "He is not here. Neither Judas nor anyone else who follows the god of that other world can ever be here."

Lazarus wanted more. "What happened to him then?"

"He has his own eternity one without hope or consolation. But your eyes are being wiped clean. You will have no recollection of any of this. Time no longer exists. What happened in the past is gone. Only this is real. The rest was lost in that dimension you knew as time."

Lazarus heard the words and in an instant Judas and all unpleasantness disappeared from his mind.

Jesus spoke again. "One day soon as man understands time though not when man expects I will return for those who know me and bring them to this place. Until then all mankind will enter through the same door you did. It is such a short trip yet it is so hard for man to take often taken in fear and doubt. They need not." Jesus smiled at his friend. "*I Am* their salvation."

Lazarus experienced the wondrous presence of the Trinity. He understood at last.

Made in the USA
Coppell, TX
07 December 2019